Love's Dawn

Love's Dawn

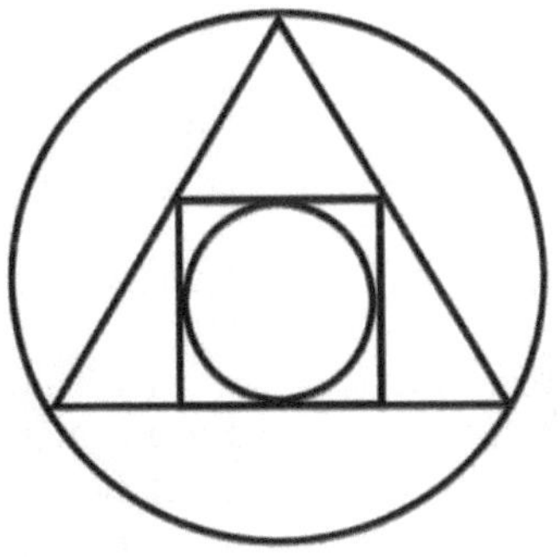

Andrew Chiniche

Reflective
Light
Press

Love's Dawn by Andrew Chiniche
Published by Reflective Light Press

First Edition: September 2018
Printed in the United States of America

Library of Congress Control Number: 2018954993

Paperback ISBN: 978-1-7326824-0-5
Hardback ISBN: 978-1-7326824-1-2
E-book ISBN: 978-1-7326824-2-9

Edited by Evy Zen
Cover by Manuela Serra

For My Muse,

The Catalyst of My Creativity.

Argument

Two intertwined souls travel

on time's ripple

like a pebble dropped in a pool.

Their journey leads to love, passion,

and worship.

Contents

Part II - *Ripples from Dawn*

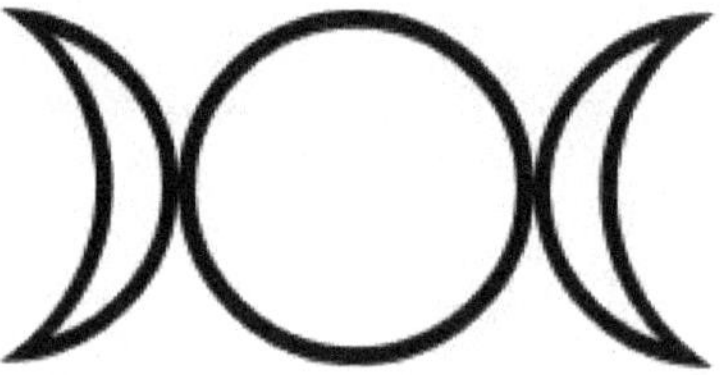

Goddess Worship

Love the maiden,
Praise the mother,
Respect the crone,
Worship the Goddess.

The triple Goddess lives in you;
You embody her power.

I want to worship at your altar;
Sacrificing you on my sword.

Gazing into your golden eyes,
I see infinite love;
Burning desire.

Your touch ignites me;
Bringing life to my soul.

Worshipping at your temple,
I've been searching for you all my life.
Let me be your dominant servant,
and fulfill your basest desires.

Reaching exalted heights,
we gaze into the eye of God and smile,
for together,
we have merged into one.

Part I

Love's Dawn

I.   *Love's Dawn*

-1888-

Feeling nervous,
despondent,
seeking an escape.

I pull aside the curtains
and peer through warped glass,
windows coated with hoarfrost.

As twilight fades,
street lamps radiate hazy light,
golden globes in the fog.

People saunter about,
huddled against the chill,
absorbed in their lives.

Donning my homburg and greatcoat,
I spring down the stairs...
The city awaits!

The first hansom passes,
then the second,
(Never take one of the first two)
I hail the third
with two fingers in the air and a whistle.

Not knowing where to go,
we rattle aimlessly along,
lanes and cobbled streets drift by.

The cabbie,
exasperated by my lack of focus,
scowls at the back of my head.

Coming to a decision,
I convey the destination,
rapping my cane for emphasis.

Eschewing Whitechapel,
we arrive at Westminster,
across from the Charing Cross Hotel.

Hopping out of the hansom,
I flip the cabbie a sovereign,
sending him on his way.

Recessed in a dark alcove,
a deep mahogany door awaits,
carved with spirals, hexagrams, stars and crescents,
highlighted with gold leaf.

(Some say it's a den of iniquity,
but they are not among the enlightened.)

Tugging the silken bell pull,
a series of chimes resonates,
calling the doorman.

Gaining admittance,
I deposit my hat and coat with the girl
and head to the Stranger's room.

I lounge on a leather settee,
close to the fire,
out of the way.

Summoning the green fairy,
Queen of Wormwood,
I place a sugar cube on the absinthe spoon,
slowly dissolving it into the green liquid.

Two drops of laudanum in the glass,
and one on the tongue;
The green fairy loves chasing the dragon.

As my senses sharpen to a razor sheen,
my thoughts absorb the universe;
A vision of beauty materializes out of the gloom.

The shoulders of a rich carmine gown
drape with a moon-bright shawl
as straight flaxen hair flows over the collar
framing a pale oval face and pouting ruby lips;
Golden amber eyes pierce my soul.

As my vision tunnels,
my brain swoons.

A lace-enclosed hand extends towards me
and sweet music falls upon my ears:

"Hello.
I am Lola.
May I sit?"

The earth reforms around me,
and reality reaffirms its grasp.

Remembering myself,
with a low bow, I stand in greeting
and take your hand in mine,
brushing my lips over your knuckles,
"Yes, please do.
The pleasure is mine."

Our conversation ebbs and flows;
Sweet nothings whisper between us.

Sitting in a comfortable silence,
your left hand cradles firmly in mine;
I feel your internal heat pulse
with your heart's contractions.

As the evening erodes,
the comfort of the settee
and the glow of the fire
begins to feel too exposed.

With intertwined hands,
we move towards the back of the building,
up the staircase, to a secluded room.

Locking the door behind us,
we're finally alone,
decorum left on the lower level.

Passion explodes in a cascade of kisses;
shedding our clothes we explore baser pleasures.

With our evening ending,
we solidify our connection
using an ancient binding ritual.

Grasping a sharpened stylus,
you intake a quick breath
as I prick your ring finger,
and then you pierce mine.

Our blood intermingles
as warm droplets drip
(drip, drip, plop)
into a crimson puddle,
pooling into a golden dish.

Taking a fountain pen in hand
life's ink draws into the nib;
We write our names onto an enchanted parchment,
a rite of interlocking calligraphy.

Held over a candle's flame,
the paper smolders,
each corner catching;
Fire licks around the edges
burning fiber to a powdery ash
and settles into the golden bowl.

The dawn breaks,
and I open the window sash
with the wind blowing off the Thames.

We hold the bowl in the breeze
and its contents swirl into the air.

As the ashes float away,
we join together in the universe;
Burnt embers scattered over love's dawn.

II.   *Yes, Mistress*

As your servant sprawls across the chaise lounge, waiting,
you glide through the doorway with a feline grace.
The wall sconces give a soft flicker.

Handmaiden of the Moon,
gleaming and radiant with a hazy sheen,
you've come to bestow an accolade.

Fumbling to my feet,
I stand to attention
and await your pleasure.

Initiating an impassioned embrace,
I hold you for protection,
desperate to be loved.

Chosen as a sacrifice by the Elders,
you grasp my hand
and lead me to the sky chamber.

The pregnant moon streams through the ceiling aperture,
pouring over an alabaster altar,
causing it to glimmer in an otherworldly light.

As I lay supine on the altar,
you bind each of my arms:
hemp rope through iron rings,
weaving mystical patterns into sacral knots.

Holding my shirt by the collar,
you rip outward;
Buttons bursts from the strain,
exposing vulnerable flesh.

Anointing my head and chest with oil,
scented Myrrh flows,
puddling on the altar,
preparing for the rite of binding.

Parted lips join.
Your tongue slides into my mouth,
and we exchange breath in passion's kiss.

Leaving teeth impressions on my neck,
your tongue traces ancient moon runes into my skin,
moving down my chest to my belly.

Navigating the intricacies of my belt buckle,
your nimble fingers open the cloth enclosure,
freeing me from my confinement.

Straddling over me,
supported by your knees,
you open your white samite robe,
letting it fall to the floor.

The moon glistens on your naked body:
Pink nipples stand to attention,
stomach muscles flex,
your sex swollen.

The Goddess has entered her servant,
power and grace radiate throughout your body.

You guide my throbbing mass past your nether lips,
penetrating to your molten core.

With a locomotive rhythm,
your body rises and falls on my piston;
The expanding intensity causes
your cheeks and chest to become flush.

As your fingers dig into my flesh,
your breath rapidly shortens
and your eyes roll back to their whites.

Magick materializes.
Lunar and erotic energies burn over us
and our bodies become electric.

Shuddering in mirrored climaxes,
a psychic dagger forms out of the ether.

Reaching from my chest with your hands,
You grasp the hilt;
The moon blade pulsates with a ghostly chill.

Screaming a berserker yell,
Frenzied downward thrusts
flay flesh from the bone.

As layers peel away,
a pink mist drifts.

Shoving your hands into my chest,
you wrap fingers around my heart,
ripping it from the captivity of its cavity.

"Take it,
possess it,
for it's always yours!"

My spirit transcends the physical:
Exposed, raw, and pulsating in the world,
swirling in chaotic parabolas.

Holding my beating heart to your chest
whilst speaking the ancient incantation,
the atmosphere implodes
in an explosion of light and sound,
and our spirits fuse together.

Two souls tether across time and space,
Anima and Animus restore their balance
and fulfill the will of the Elders.

III.   *Cosmos in a Sunbeam*

As a sunbeam streams on my face,
a cosmos of dust particles
floats through a broken blind;
I greet the afternoon
with bleary eyes and a cotton mouth.

Reaching for the water pitcher,
I brush my fingers on the handle.

Pain pulses up my left hand
recalling the night's pleasures:
Flash of golden eyes,
Moaning of ruby lips,
Trembling of ecstatic flesh.

Staring at my wounded finger
freshly bloodied from bruising the scab,
the rite of dawn replays through my mind.

Exhausted from the expenditure of Magick,
we lose our grasp on the bowl
and it plummets towards the earth.

As I stretch out trying to grab hold,
she swiftly draws back.

With a final lunge, I grapple the bowl
and reel it to my chest;
Collapsing back into the room,
I heap on the floor.

Catching my breath and my bearings,
my eyes glance about,
the hallway visible through the open door.

In her hasty retreat,
Lola has left the door ajar
and her shawl behind.

Pushing away the disappointment
of her departure,
I pour a glass of water.

The crisp clear liquid saturates my mouth,
chasing away the fairy's green fog,
clearing my head.

Dragging myself out of bed,
I trudge into the sitting room.

Plopping down on the tufted armed tatum,
I grab my coat;
Digging through the front pocket,
I pull out Lola's shawl.

Made of a shimmering silvery white silk,
it captures the light of the full moon.

Holding it by the corners
and extending my arms,
I expose the full rectangle length;
A strange weight droops at the center.

Turning the shawl around,
I discover a secret pocket sewn on,
a hard round object enclosed inside.

Grabbing my pen knife,
I remove the stitching across the pocket's mouth,
and a hidden token rolls across my palm:
Sovereign size,
made of polished brass.

On the obverse,
etched along the top and bottom:
ET DELECTUS GRADUM - QUAERETIS ME
(You are selected for the next level - Search for me)
An all-seeing eye at the center.

On the reverse,
A circle in a square in a triangle:
"Squaring the circle."
An alchemist's glyph,
Symbol of the philosopher's stone.

After being a casual member of the Society for years,
I've been chosen for a higher purpose.
My path to enlightenment begins,
and Lola is the gateway.

IV. *Lady of Luminous Aura*

I

As I reach for the psychic dagger suspended above me,
electric orgasmic energy radiates through my body.
Your spent seed cascades from my receptacle,
running down my inner thigh.

Screaming a berserker yell
I attack with a frenzy,
flaying flesh.
Blood droplets populate my skin,
highlighting my flaxen hair with a pink mist.

As I take your life,
alchemy roots in my womb.
I am your lover and your mother.
We have created the future.

With a final downward thrust,
double fists around the dagger's hilt,
your sternum splits
and your chest opens;
Your heart beats slowly
between your deflating lungs.

I shove both hands into the cavity,
lovingly caressing your heart,
ripping, tugging, pulling.
Your muscle pulses as it's lifted from its captivity.

Held above my head,
moonlight swirls in concentric circles.

As I hold your beating heart to my chest,
blood smears on my hard nipples,
and I chant an ancient incantation:

"Rogo Deam luna!
Offero tibi sacrificium hoc mundo.
Liga anima una; ad vitam restituit statera."

(I call upon the moon Goddess!
I offer this sacrifice to you and the universe.
Bind our souls together; restore balance to life.)

Blue transitioning into white:
Your life's light exits your eyes
and drifts into the sky,
encircling the moon in a hazy halo.

As our spirits fuse together,
my soul distorts.
Agony rips through me bodily;
The atmosphere implodes
in an explosion of light and sound,

and ...
(with a gasp)
... I am awake,
my pillow sopping with sweat.

A reoccurring fever dream,
reliving a past life,
grows with intensity since my Becoming.

Souls tethered for millennia,
come hurling across time and space;
All the portents point towards the Drawing.

II

A bloodline traced to the beginnings of patriarchal rule:
The Mother priestess struck down by the Warrior king.
His power asserted through rape and slaughter.
Life's balance disrupted.

Driven underground,
the Goddess cult continued practicing in secret,
cloaked by night under the moon's illumination.
Maiden, Mother, and Crone kept the rites living
and the generations growing stronger.

Conceived by the light of a full moon
and nurtured in the womb,
Earth's power surrounds me.

During the apex of each month's rotation,
the Goddess radiates in me;
My mother's belly glows red
with skin taut like a drum.

On the Vernal Equinox,
I enter the world at midnight
through blood, mucus, and pain,
absorbing my mother's life as my own.
A birth caul muffles my cries.

Baring the mark of the Goddess on my shoulder—
a circle flanked by two crescents—
The moon coven adopts me.

A child of delight
and days of daisy chains,
I live in a pastoral paradise.

During my thirteenth twelvemonth,
as I crested my favorite hillock,
a blood moon rose.

In praise of the Goddess
and remembrance of my mother,
I bow my head to mutter a prayer.

Suddenly,
collapsing to ground,
my eyes roll to their whites.

Past lives open up
as knowledge bubbles from time's hold.
Visions explode through my optic nerves:

Dancing in a fairy ring;
Crying of a colicky baby;
Burning plague ravaged victims;
Cold steel opening a raver's throat;
Thrashing body held underwater;
Love's passion erupting.

A bright red line of agony
twists in my intestines,
ripping from my crotch to my brain,
tearing me in two.

Struggling to keep myself together,
I wrap my arms around,
holding on like a vise,
trying to survive.

Slowly the pain tapers,
becoming a dull ache.
My past lives recede,
imbedding into the recesses of my brain.

A sense of normalcy returns
as I notice a surprising warm wetness
spreading between my legs.

Moving my hand to where my legs meet,
I tenderly probe with my fingers.

In the orb's light,
they are maroon with a viscous liquid.

The arrival of my moon's flow
fulfills the blood covenant.
The Goddess reaffirms her hold upon me.

Childhood pleasures,
A recent memory,
My maidenhood begins.

III

During the preceding twenty years,
I have endured many complex trials and rituals;
Past life lessons resurfaced
and their knowledge ingrained into my psyche.

With my mind and body honed to a razor sharpness,
I am an instrument for the Goddess' bidding.

On the brink of my destiny,
a final ordeal awaits.

Standing in the vestibule
behind two heavily grained oak doors:
Sound vibrates.

Harmonizing choral voices
sing praise to the Goddess
and her emissary, the moon.

To distract the nervous energy building in my body,
I gaze at a polished full-length mirror of bronze:

A crown of woven willows rests upon my brow
as an iron collar graces my neck,
a braided leash dangles down;
My wrists' shackles attach to heavy chains
that hang to the floor in piles.

A mouse-color hopsack shift
hangs loosely against my body;
The hem to the top of my knees,
sleeves just short of the shackles.

Standing with bare feet
on a time-worn floor,
a chill courses through my body.

KREEEEK!

The sky chamber's massive doors open,
startling me out of my reverie;
The time of my Becoming has arrived.

The chorus of praise devolves
into an agonizing chant,
Volume increases to deeper decibels.

Two male servants wearing loincloths,
their features hidden by blank masks,
grab the chains hanging from my wrists
and jerks the leash.

Resisting the forward momentum,
I am dragged up the ash-coated aisle.
Powdered clouds rise at each heavy step.
The chanting increases in its aggressive tone
and reverberates around my body.

Moonlight pours through the ceiling aperture,
lighting up the dais;
Two Doric columns await my installation.

As I fight and resist,
sweat runs down my face,
its saltiness stinging my eyes,
but it's to no avail.

They carry me up the dais,
forcing me into position between the columns
and turn me to face the jeering crowd.

The priest of the horned god stands before me
wearing a ram's head and royal purple vestments.

Barking orders at his servants,
they take hold of the sides of my shift
and pull with flexing arms,
ripping it along the seams,

leaving me naked
and vulnerable to the world,
but bathed in the Goddess' light.

Click! Click! Click! Click!
Chains thread through giant iron rings,
expanding my arms into an open cross.

The horned god swings a thurible
back and forth beneath my nose;
A burning mixture of hashish and incense
billows through its openings.

The fumes force themselves upon me.
Tears flood from my irritated eyes.

Finally giving in,
I breathe deeply,
filling my lungs.

The chanting intensifies,
a suffocating hum addles my brain.

Standing behind me
with a hand at the center of my back,
the horned god pushes me forward,
bending me at the waist.

Muffled by the ram's head,
he intones an incantation;

My mind twists and tumbles,
thrown back through the mists of time.

I am the Mother priestess
in the thrall of the Warrior king.

Chains tighten on my arms
and my legs are forced apart,
fumblings around my crotch.

Against my internal desire,
my womanhood becomes wet.

Alien hands on my hips yank me back,
and air rushes between slapping flesh
as a cock rams inside me.

I scream in outrage at this violation
and the energy of the Goddess erupts!

Pulling my arms together,
tearing down the columns,
I thrust them towards the sky:
My chains and shackles explode
in a shower of debris.
The iron collar dissipates.

Above me,
formed out of the ether,
I grasp the psychic dagger.

With a frenzied yell I turn around,
driving it up to the hilt into the Warrior king.

My head clears,
My breathing calms,
My eyes open on the present.

Before me is a sacrificed ram;
A dagger protrudes from its neck
and blood squirts all over me.

As I return from the vision,
my womanhood
and body are still under my control.

Pulling the dagger from the beast,
I turn and face the coven.

The agonizing chant evolves
into a joyful song of celebration—
A chorus of praise.

The two male servants cover my nakedness,
draping me in a white samite robe.

The priest of the horned god places
a golden crown
adorned with moonstones and opals
upon my head.

With the dagger resting on the flat of my hands,
I raise it skyward towards the moon.

"Praise be to the Goddess!
Through her strength and will,
I had the power to endure this ordeal!

After my mother died during my birth,
you adopted me and raised me as your own.
Thank you for your support,
your faith in me.

All my life you have known me as Daphne.

This night,
on the anniversary of my mother's death,
I am crowned,
and reborn as Lola,
Lady of Luminous Aura!"

V. *Meditating into Memories*

I

Meditating in the lotus position,
I sit on an ancient mat of woven papyrus;
My hands held palm up,
Thumbs and forefingers pinched together.

Fragrant smoke
burning from a taper
tickles my face,
causing my eyes to squint.

As I struggle to focus my will,
sweat beads on my brow.

Entering through my third eye,
I split open my brain,
accessing its deeper depths.

A ghostly hand
opens the drawer
of my subconscious.

Taking control over the reoccurring dream,
I thread it into my mind's projector.

The perspective becomes fluid;
Watching as if from a floating eyeball.

I concentrate on the psychic dagger
lying discarded at the side of the altar—
It's gore dripping onto the porous floor.

A leather wrapped hilt attaches
to a foot-long steel blade
that gleams with a sharp sheen.
Etched moon runes glow along the blood groove
And a Burmese ruby glitters in the pommel.

Shrinking my perception,
I descend into the blade's consciousness.

Appearing at times of intense emotion,
it is ancient and beyond time,
bonded to my lives,
existing everywhen at once.

As I awaken from a deep trance,
I hover over my writing desk.

My left hand wraps around the dagger's hilt,
as the ruby glows with an internal light,
the point blooded from my right index finger.

Written on a sheet of foolscap,
Scrawled in my body's ink:
'The Elders' sacrifice has returned;
Fulfill their will and restore the balance.'

II

After a millennium,
traces of his spirit still linger,
swirling through mine.

I concentrate on the pain,
letting it fill my brain:
The dagger entering his chest,
The flaying of his flesh,
His heart being ripped out;
The distortion of my soul.

Our pain is the gateway.

To proceed in the present,
I must enter his past—
His memories fade as his life drains.

Peering through a fern bough,
over a calm pond,
she appears on the shore.

(As my cheeks glow in a warm blush,
my heart enters my throat,
and my breath catches.)

Glancing around,
thinking she's alone,
she shimmies out of her robe,
letting it fall to the beach.

Her nubile flesh glows in the afternoon light
as straight flaxen hair dangles over her budding breasts;
Her mirrored reflection bounces off the water.

With a giggle and a shivering gasp,
she plunges feet first,
splashing around.

(Love's heat blossoms through my body,
My heart reaches out to her.)

As a servant of the coven,
I've known her all my life,
but a shift has occurred in my brain,
and I'll never see her differently.

———

In the twilight between day and night,
underneath a weeping willow,
a brook bubbles at our feet.

Surrounded by a halo of lightning bugs
with nature witnessing our holy act,
we exchange secret vows.

By a small bonfire alight with flames,
I present you a hand-tied bouquet,
composed of lavender, jasmine, and lilies
with a spray of baby's breath.

"You, my love, are my moon;
Reflecting and magnifying the Goddess's light,
making everything greater in my life."

"You are the sun of my universe,
Life sustaining and brightening my darkness.
Through you I've discovered my worth."

Gazing into each other's eyes,
our intertwined hands hold the bouquet,
and we throw it into the fire;
We breathe in the fragrant smoke deeply.

Anointing our heads in myrrh
and tracing a unifying circle,
we make our vow:

"My life is yours and I give it all.
Everything I do, and everything I am
is dedicated to you.

Together we grow in love—
through this life and beyond."

Taking you in my arms,
I swoop you back,
and breathe in your breath,
concluding the ceremony with passion's kiss.

I lead us deep into the forest
to a fairy ring carved out of the surrounding trees.
Our marriage bed awaits under the stars.

Virgin bodies explore one another
and we consummate our union.

As the coming of dawn
pierces through the trees,
we awaken from a satisfying slumber,
tired and bathed in dew.

After helping each other dress,
we walk hand-in-hand,
floating on a cloud of bliss
and exit to the meadow
that borders the forest.

With a bodily shock,
I am tackled and pushed to the earth,
squirming under an unknown muscular weight.

I watch you fight to pull away,
screaming to be free.
A pair of priestess pin you
and hold you by the arms.

As they stand up,
dragging you away,
you yell out,
"Artus!"

Trying to respond,
a squeak of sound escapes my mouth
as pain explodes from the back of my head.

All I know is darkness.

With a throbbing skull,
I awake lying on a cot in a cell,
fresh straw scattered over the floor.
The afternoon light angles through a window.

In the corner,
in the shadows,
a hooded figure squats on a stool,
head down as if in prayer.

Hearing me shuffle around,
the figure begins to speak
with an ancient voice:

"Do not be afraid.
Forgive us for your maltreatment.
It was a necessary step towards
accomplishing the wishes of the Elders.

Your illicit affair
and secret union with Dafnee,
while frowned upon,
has fulfilled its purpose.

You need to keep her love in your heart.
She will be cared for
and will resume her training.

When the time comes,
you will be called for and rewarded.
We will honor the sacrifice you have made.

You will stay here in this cell
where your needs will be accounted for,
and you will continue your service to the coven."

With these final words,
the hooded figure collapses upon itself
with a whisper of fabric,
leaving an empty cloak piled on a stool.

After two and a third twelvemonth,
the call came.

Dressed in the finest of silks and linens,
I am lead to an antechamber.

As I sprawl across the chaise lounge, waiting,
you glide through the doorway with a feline grace.
The wall sconces give a soft flicker.

Handmaiden of the Moon,
gleaming and radiant with a hazy sheen,
you've come to bestow an accolade.

VI. *Initiation into Dawn*

Over fourteen centuries,
the moon coven remained hidden,
keeping the significant bloodlines intact,
but its existence fading,
dying along with its members.

As the Colonies rebelled,
breaking away from the Crown,
The Society of the Lunar Dawn began
with a twofold purpose:
to expand the coven's influence,
and the recruitment of raw talent.

After gaining a member's confidence,
a recommendation is made,
and your name is submitted for review.

Standing before the Tribunal,
all qualifications are tallied;
Passing their scrutiny,
you endure the Rite of Beginnings.

As the new moon dawns,
and renews its life cycle,
night pours through the windows;
Candles flicker in their sconces,
dim light surrounded by darkness.

Alone at the entrance,
absorbing the atmosphere,
a hand rests on your shoulder
sending a shiver down your spine.

The arrival of your sponsor
signals the beginning of the rite.

Tying a crimson scarf across your eyes,
you are blind to the past,
and freely enter the guild hall
to seek a new path.

As a disembodied voice
reads from the Book of Morgaina,
you follow with slow deliberate steps.

*"After my defilement,
I awake but cannot see.
Everything is black
with my body swollen,
and radiating pain."*

Walking twenty-nine and a half steps,
symbolically traveling the lunar cycle,
you begin in darkness to arrive in the light.

*"Once embedded in stone
and held aloft as a unifying symbol,
Now restored to my care,
An object of psychic power."*

Stepping into the final half-step,
a sharp pain pierces
as a rapier enters your breast—
Not deeply but drawing blood,
Representing the pain of rebirth.

"Like Lilith before me,
an outcast and survivor,
I am connected to the earth;
My progeny destined to expand."

With your right hand over the wound,
the blade protruding through your fingers,
you recite the oath of fidelity:

"Reborn in blood,
standing before the newly risen moon,
I embrace its ancient wisdom.
With this bond I swear allegiance
to The Society of the Lunar Dawn,
accepting its guidance."

Untying the silk scarf
and folding it into a square,
you wipe the withdrawn blade clean,
and let the scarf fall into a flaming brazier.

"Brought to Avalon
Dying from his son's death stroke,
Arthur's placed on a pyre,
Rejoining the universe;
He will return again."

The ashes float upward,
through an aperture in the ceiling,
towards the new moon.

The rite complete.
Your sponsor embraces you,
offering welcome to a novice member.

VII. *Warden of the Moon*

I

Thirty years after beginning my journey,
I am promoted to a position of authority:
Warden of the Moon.

Of the five membership tiers to ascend,
the first three open to everyone,
while the last two, the most important,
are a whispered secret.

Through the progression of years,
tests and rituals exist to entertain and amuse;
Seeming exotic and mysterious,
and, for some, fulfilling sexual peculiarities.

Scattered among these hollow practices,
core rituals distinguish the worthy.

These particular members exhibit traits
and knowledge whose origins
flow from past bloodlines,
qualifying them for promotion.

After being elevated to the elite tiers,
a choice is made:
Serve the Society in the city
or self-exile to the hidden temple.

II

As a member of the highest tier,
it is my duty to protect the coven.

Through studying the Chronicles,
accumulating rare artifacts,
and overseeing the Society's membership,
the larger picture reveals itself.

Throughout life and history
patterns repeat, multiply, and overlap,
rippling through time's pond,
expanding outward in concentric circles
and signaling when great occurrences arrive.

In the records of the coven,
two notable souls have existed:
Born during the fourth century,
they brought about the great kingdom,
and were instrumental in its collapse.

Intertwined, they belong together,
and all signs point to their reemergence.

III

Walking with a regal air,
surrounded by a cloud of mystery,
Lola floats into my office.

As head priestess of the coven,
she focuses on less mundane concerns,
and rarely visits the Society.

"Warden, I bring you greetings and salutations
along with congratulations on your recent promotion.
The coven appreciates your efforts,
and we expect greatness in the future.

During the last two months,
meditating over a reoccurring dream,
I have connected with a former life.

Two souls—
Anima and Animus—
Bound through a traumatic experience,
have returned to this plane,
and I'm searching for the male aspect.

He associated with the coven in the past,
but his presence has not reappeared;
I have come to seek him at the Society."

Leaving my office
and walking down the hall,
we enter the records room:
Files stack from floor to ceiling
with a table and chair at the center.

Withdrawing an ancient dagger
from beneath her robes,
she wraps both hands around the hilt,
and with a muffled grunt,
drives it into the table top.

The ruby in the pommel
flickers in time with the gas lights.

I recognize this famous artifact
from its descriptions in the annals.

According to legend
the dagger was once part of the sword
used by the once and future King.

Sitting at the head of the table
with the dagger standing before her,
she closes her eyes,
moving her hands in patterns
around the pommel—
circles, spirals, and figure eights—
and chanting in a low tone.

With faster movements and tighter forms,
the ruby glows with a bright hue.
The red light focuses into a beam,
projecting into the center of the room.

Slapping her hands together,
the beam splatters,
Concentrating in one area.

Arising, she moves to the drawer stack,
and, upon opening,
finds one file glimmering a dull ruby red.

"Having tasted him during a binding ritual,
the dagger connects with his being,
and is drawn towards items he has handled."

Pulling the file
and laying it open on the table,
she reveals a certificate of membership
signed after his Initiation:

Arthur Pragon.

VIII. *Evening of the Equinox*

The sky over the Thames
transforms from inky black,
with light seeping around the horizon
into a full blaze.

Sitting on a balcony
I enjoy the calm, cool morning
as the Autumn Equinox arrives.

Tonight, I complete the Drawing,
reuniting our bodies,
and initiating his journey to the past.

As twilight fades,
I close my eyes.
Going deeper into myself,
I call him towards me.

Utilizing our connection,
time flows around me.
I imagine the journey here,
pulling him with my mind.

Riding in a hansom
we arrive at a deep mahogany door,
carved with ritualistic symbols,
located in a dark alcove.

Releasing my hold,
I wait, gathering my strength.

After a soft rap-tap tapping
on my chamber door,
I open my eyes.
"Yes, please enter."

"Mistress,
the gentleman has arrived.
He relaxes in the Stranger's room
near the fireplace."

"Very well.
Thank you.
You may leave me."

Rising to my feet,
I gaze in a mirror:
Wearing a rich carmine gown
with my hair flowing to the collar,
I drape a moon-bright shawl over my shoulders.

A brass token hidden inside,
embossed with an alchemist's glyph,
will lead him on his future quest
towards transmutation.

Leaving my boudoir
and descending the stairs,
I stand in the doorway
and gaze around the room.

Wooden walls paneled like ebony night
gleam with firelight as it flickers in the hearth.
A smoky cigar haze hangs in the air.

Conversations murmur,
droning like a hive
and divulging secrets.

Since our last union ended
with his sacrifice by my hand,
I feel a nervous fluster,
my stomach flipping.

Filling my lungs with a calming breath,
the room descends into silence
and I walk over.

At the leather settee where he lounges,
I extend a lace-enclosed hand
and make my introduction:

"Hello.
I am Lola.
May I sit?"

His eyes dilate,
surprised by my approach,
and confusion abounds
before he focuses on me.

Standing with a low bow,
he takes my hand in greeting,
brushing his lips over my knuckles.
"Yes, please do.
The pleasure is mine.
I am Art to my friends."

As we talk about nothing,
exploring our personalities,
I take his hand in mine
and look into his eyes—
A stormy sea of grayish blue.

I feel our past bubbling
below the surface,
ready to crest
and flow into the present.

I move until my lips almost touch his ear,
and with a breathless whisper:
"Whilst we are comfortable here,
it feels too exposed.

Would you like to continue
our tête-à-tête upstairs?"

His lips spread into a grin,
and, with a glimmer in his eyes,
his head gives a positive nod.

Arising and holding my hand,
he helps me to my feet.
With his arm around my waist,
we move towards the back of the building,
up the staircase,
and I direct him to a secluded room.

Locking the door behind us,
we are finally alone.

Pulling my shawl off my shoulders,
I drop it on the floor.
And, with my hands on his chest,
I push him to the sofa.

Locking eyes,
golden flowing into blue,
I loosen the buttons of my dress,
opening the bodice
and shed it like a second skin.

Reaching behind my back,
I untie my skirt at the waist
and let it drift to the floor.

In my lace camisole and knickers,
I saunter over and straddle him,
bending forward till our lips join.

Taking his tongue into my mouth,
I move my hips in circular patterns.
A hardness grows in his lap
in response to my sucking and grinding.

As he peals my camisole over my head,
my nipples spring up—
hard towers in the chilly air.

Using his ears as handles,
I guide his head,
moving his mouth over my breast.

As he seals his lips around,
tongue flicking the fleshy tower,
warmth spreads from my chest,
to the base of my brain,
swirling and ebbing through my body
until it concentrates in my swollen sex.

He reaches to his trousers,
attempting to release himself,
and I halt his hand.
"The time is not yours.
You will allow me my pleasure."

"Yes, Mistress."

Sliding out of my under clothes,
naked, I stand on the sofa,
and lower my nether lips over his mouth.

Penetrating me with his tongue,
he sups at my chalice,
telling his story with intense motion.

A shutter vibrates through my being,
and a moan escapes my throat
as he coaxes me into orgasm.

My spent body melts into his arms,
and we hold each other.
Memories of Artus and the fairy ring
float through my mind.

Our evening ending,
dawn on the verge of breaking,
we solidify our connection
using an ancient binding ritual.

He grasps a sharpened stylus,
and I intake a quick breath
as he pricks my ring finger,
and then I pierce his.

Our blood intermingles
as warm droplets drip
(drip, drip, plop)
into a crimson puddle,
pooling into a golden dish.

As he struggles with the bowl,
I make my escape,
bounding down the stairs
and out the front door.

Climbing aboard a waiting carriage,
I embark for the coven,
The Drawing complete.

Souls fused through violence
a thousand years past,
reunite with a small bloodletting.

IX.   *Quest for the Chalice*

I

As I walk around the streets of London,
the brass token lying heavy in my pocket,
thoughts of Lola comfort me
with an expanse of centuries connecting us.

Ever since our night together,
my consciousness has expanded,
moving beyond the nearby universe
and reaching into the past.

Turning onto Candleswick Street,
a bedraggled park lies hidden:
Peering through an overgrown hedgerow
with tangled brambles blocking the gate.

I push my way into the green.
Thorns rip flesh through my trousers
causing blood to drip down my leg.

With a step onto a worn flagstone path,
a mist begins to swirl about me
blocking out the sun.

I follow where it spirals,
leading me towards the center,
where a large stone perches on a mound.

On the outskirts of my peripheral vision,
intentionally avoiding my direct sight,
an uproar of beasts assaults my hearing—
Their cries and howls pierce my mind.

From my studies at the Society,
I realize that I have wandered
into a sacred hollow—
A window carved out of reality,
exposing what a wayfarer needs to see.

As I plod forward,
pushing myself towards momentum,
my steps gain weight
like treading through glue.

The oxygen thins
and the atmosphere thickens,
slowing my progress.

Fighting for every inch,
my muscles burn—
Their energy depletes
with each stride forward.

On the edge of exhaustion,
I round the spiral,
and begin my ascent up the mound,
when I pause in my struggle.

Before me two creatures—
both existing in books of legend—
stand by to repel interlopers.

Muscular legs coil like taunt springs
with a scorpion stinger set to strike.
A manticore lies ready.

While a gryphon preens its wings,
meticulously grooming each feather,
appearing to be oblivious to my presence
except for its continuously tracking eyes.

With a burning warmth,
a vibrating heat erupts,
pushing me into action.

Reaching with my hand,
I pull out the token.
Slowly opening my fist,
it lies on the flat of my palm—
the obverse side up.

The all-seeing eye opens wide
and a vibrant white light pours out,
dispelling the gloom and mist.

In between my thumb and forefinger,
I hold the object over my head
with the eye facing forward.

Both creatures step back three paces,
appearing to bow as they do so,
allowing me to pass
and access the mound.

Climbing next to the mysterious stone,
shaped as an oblong cylinder
and carved from pure white marble,
an impression divots the top.

In a flash of instinct,
I fit the brass token vertically in the slot,
and it descends to a halfway point,
clicking into place.

Time falls around me.
My surroundings twist in a kaleidoscope
with a torrent of rainbow colors
turning me inside out.

As I emerge from the trance,
my hands wrap around
the handle of a great sword.
A ruby glows in the pommel
with the blade imbedded in stone.

Feeling a current of flowing energy,
I yell like a Norse warrior
and pull the sword's handle:
Sparks fly as steel screams against marble,
The blade leaves its prison.

Etched moon runes
run along the blood grove,
reflecting the transcendent orb
as I hold the sword over my head
and become aware of my surroundings.

An army of knights, squires,
and men-at-arms kneel before me,
saluting and chanting:
"All hail the King!
Long live King Arthur!
All hail King Arthur!
Long live the King!"

II

Awakening next to the stone,
shivering as the night's chill settles in,
I grab the edge and pull myself up.

With the vision fresh in my mind,
echoes of the chant bounce in my head
like a child's round.

I retrieve the token from the slot,
appearing, for the moment, spent,
and amble my way across the park,
ignoring the flagstone path.

Hailing a hansom
(always the third one)
I travel to my flat.

Disturbed by my afternoon,
I decide to stay in for the evening.

Concocting an elderberry wine mixture,
with a heavy dose of laudanum
to smooth out the edges,
I sit in my great chair
staring at a stain-glass grate.

As the fire makes the colors dance,
I contemplate what I saw.

Becoming mesmerized
I drift to the past again,
revisiting a life once lived.

With my recently won sword in hand,
I hurry to the aid of King Leodegrance.

After professing his allegiance to me,
he quickly became besieged by opposing forces.

Leading my men into the fray,
slicing and hacking flesh all around,
the temporary enemy is trounced
and beaten into submission.

With my blood running hot
from the lust of battle,
I glance to the top of the castle wall
where a beauty stands by a turret
surveying the field of slaughter.

To reward my help,
and strengthen the kingdom,
Leodegrance calls me over.

"My liege lord,
I give you thanks for subduing
the forces sieging my keep
and freeing us from their captivity.

As a token of my appreciation,
I introduce you to my daughter, Guinevere.
(winking and a nodding to the crowd)
And who knows?
A young king might want a beautiful wife."

While everyone laughs at his joke,
I knew that I found my queen.

At that same instance,
in protest to my decision,
a sharp pain strikes my deep psyche -
An intertwined soul makes herself known.

III

Sailing around the northern isles,
the sea brews into a tempest.

As the wind shears through the sails,
tearing them to shreds,
the hull smashes into shards
against the rocks with a crack of timber.

Washing up on shore,
inert like a bloated corpse,
I sink into the porous beach
as treacherous waves ebb and flow,
covering me in a wet blanket.

I hear feet being sucked into sand
as someone walks around me.

A muffled voice issues a command,
and I am lifted into a prone position.
Water rushes off me,
and I am carried away.

Awakening in a darkened chamber,
a fire crackles in the hearth
as a furnace cooks beneath my skin:
A fever torments my body
with alternate waves of freezing shivers,
and shimmering heat.

Moonlight seeps through the window,
and a Goddess appears before me,

surrounded by a pale aura
with cascading auburn hair
flowing over her shoulders.

I watch her lips part,
and her words drift to my ears,
caressing me with their kisses.

"Arthur,
I am here for you.
We will complete our circuit
and reunite our intertwined souls."

Moving as if in a dream,
she reaches to her waist,
sensually untying her robe.

Undressing with a deliberate motion,
she teases me with her slowness,
before letting her raiment drift to the floor.

An angelic vision,
her body beckons me.

My eyes follow her curves:
traveling from her hips,
dancing at her lips
to arrive at her breasts,
where each nipple,
like pink rose petals,
highlights her milky flesh.

Gravity pulls my gaze downward,
over her firm stomach,
around her cute belly button
to become enraptured:
Her womanhood in full flower,
crowned with a fiery bush.

Stripping back my covers,
she reveals my fever-racked body,
naked except for a sheen of sweat.

Although I lie on the bed,
I stand at attention—
One part not betrayed by sickness.

With a knowing smirk,
she crawls over my body,
and our flesh feeds one another.

Her smooth velvet heat encases me,
enveloping me in a liquid tightness.

Her fingers dig into my chest
as the steady rhythm of her hips
causes her breathing to become ragged.

Leaning forward,
with her lips at my ear,
she whispers,
"Fill my womb....
I want your essence dripping out of me!"

In an involuntary reaction to her words,
I give a final spasmodic thrust,
exploding inside her.

Her body grinds to a halt,
and she lies on top of me,
breathing a satisfied sigh.

"Thank you.
You have given me our son
and the means of your death.

Now sleep...
Remember nothing...
Awake refreshed and revitalized."

As I drift off to sleep,
she slides back into her robe
and pulls the bed clothes over me.

In time with the arrival of Morpheus' gift,
she leans over me and bestows a blessing
with a lover's kiss.

Awakening in a sun drenched room,
a soft breeze drifts through the window.

The aroma of a strong broth
wafts into my nose
as my vigilant nurse maid
holds a spoon to my lips.

Noticing my eyes open,
she calls to the doorway:
"Fetch the mistress!
Our guest awakes."

My hostess glides through the doorway,
walking with a feline grace.

"My Lord Arthur,
my heart soars to see you recovering!

Welcome to the Kingdom of Orkney.
I am Morgaina."

"How did I come to be here?"

"A quick gale surfaced.
Your ship rapidly capsized,
throwing you ashore.

After the shipwreck,
a brain fever struck you,
and for the past fortnight,
you have been under my watch."

"My dear lady,
we thank you for your care and fidelity.

How fairs the remainder of my crew?"

"I wish t'were different,
but tragedy struck that evening...
You were the only survivor."

"That is disheartening.
Those were brave, honest men
who had no peer in the realm.

(After a moments contemplation...)

Please excuse my ignorance;
I know we have never met,
but I seem to recognize you."

"That is easily explained.

On the night of your birth,
you were whisked away—
But not before imprinting
your mother's face into your memory.
T'is her that you recognize in me."

"How is that possible?"

"Because, my dear King,
I am your sister,
or rather, half-sister,
as my father is my own,
but not yours.

As befits siblings,
and because we are well-met,
you may call me Anna."

IV

The betrayal of my wife
with my best friend
rests heavily on my soul,
and I cannot fathom the act.

Sinking into a deep depression,
the despair and darkness inside me
oozes into the realm.

Monsters, human and otherworldly,
roam around terrorizing my subjects
as the enlightenment of Camelot
dims along with the old ways.

The growing anguish
allowed the religion of the Christ
to seep into my people's lives,
promising a release from suffering,
and a hope of everlasting life.

Although I am not convinced of its vitality,
most of the fellowship subscribes
to the new teachings,
and I allow the rituals to continue.

During the high holy days,
we meet at the Round Table
regaling each other with tales
and embellishments of our past quests;
A window to happier times.

On this feast of Whitsunday,
the table is not complete,
for Lancelot's seat lies vacant.

After the discovery of his affair,
he exiled himself to Brittany
to flagellate in penance.

Although I cannot forgive him for the act,
his seat remains his and will remain empty.
He paid for it in blood many times over,
and I am loyal to the memory of our friendship.

At the culmination of our noon repast,
an ominous wind roars from the west,
as the moon emerges to blot out the sun,
darkening the great hall in a dismal light.

With a resounding thunderclap,
a brilliantly glowing chalice materializes,
suspended over the center of table,
and replaces the hidden sun with its ethereal light.

"My lordships,
the holy grail has appeared before you.

To save your King and Camelot,
you must undertake this quest:
Locate the cup of Christ,
and unburden your souls."

The vision dissipates
at the conclusion of her speech,
and the previously unseen maiden,
wrapped in a snow-white shift
with hair as black as a raven,
exits the hall through a side door.

Always the first to action,
Sir Gawain stands on his chair,
balancing himself with a foot on the table,
and brandishes his sword to the sky.

"For King, Camelot and Christ,
I accept this quest!
Who is with me?"

My heart swells with pride
as my loyal men,
The Knights of the Round Table,
rise with swords raised high,
vowing to quest for the holy grail
with a resounding,
"Aye!"

V

Beginning with an enthusiastic vigor,
the grail quest continues,
but with a diminished hope
as bleak news arrives from afar.

Reports of my knights' failures—
death for some,
dismemberment for others—
strengthens the gloom that surrounds me,
weakening my health.

To bring some joy back to the kingdom,
I preside over a feast on St. Crispin's Day.

Sitting amongst my guests,
listening to their conversations,
and laughing with their jokes,
we all live for the moment.

CLA-BANG!

The main doors swing open
and a deafening silence fills the room.
A woman and her stripling enter.

Standing with some difficulty,
my limbs shake with a slight tremor.
I address the new comers:
"All are welcome on this feast day.
Please join...

Morgaina?
Is that you?

My cherished sister!
I am pleased that you have come.
Welcome to Camelot!"

"Thank you, my dear brother.

My son has come of age,
and I am here to present him to the court.

(He steps forward, bowing)

King Arthur,
this is Mordred of Orkney...
Your nephew."

Extending my hand,
I gesture to the table.
"Here, Mordred, take my chair.
Eat, be merry, and meet everyone."

"Yes, Uncle."

"Morgaina,
come with me."

I offer her the crook of my arm
and we walk to my study.
She holds me as I lean into her,
assisting me more than I guide her.

Sitting down in my favorite chair,
I offer her the adjacent seat.

"Since we last saw each other,
at least a decade has passed
with much changing in my life."

"I have heard the stories about Guinevere,
her paramour, Lancelot,
and the rumors concerning your health.

I traveled here to verify the information,
and, now, with my own eyes,
I see a deeply imbedded sickness."

"My dearest Anna,
with your insight, you see truly.

As you nursed me once before,
restoring my health,
I welcome the return of your healing touch."

"Arthur,
I will do as you bid,
restoring your missing vitality,
but I need a favor in return."

"Of course,
It is yours for the asking.
Whatsoever can I do?"

"Make Mordred a part of your court."

"I have something fitting for a boy his age.
From this moment forward, he will
assume an important role...
That of my personal page."

"Thank you, my brother.
Your nephew will serve you
as a son serves his father."

VI

Mordred became ingrained
in the mechanisms of court life,
and, if the rumors be true,
stole the hearts of many a maiden.

As he grew to the fringes of manhood,
my health improved under Morgaina's care,
and years of my youth returned.

After giving me my nightly draught,
her voice floats through the fog of my brain.
"Awake refreshed and revitalized."

And that night,
for the first time in years,
I dreamed.

Dreamed, not a nightmare,
but a dream of passion;
A dream of desire;
A dream of intertwined souls joining;
A dream of Morgaina using me as her toy.

Awakening with a spasmodic motion,
her words drift about my mind.
"You have given me our son,
and the means of your death."

Watching the predawn glow,
I knew her words
and their implication
to be true.

As the morning sun rises,
Peeking through the drapes,
I wait.

Morgaina will come soon,
so I open the curtains
and let the sun's majesty
shine through the window.

As the sun pours
past the curtains,
its heat empowers me
with its warm embrace.

"Morgaina,
my beautiful seductress,
I bid you a good morning."

"Arthur,
whatever do you mean?"

"After all these years,
I now know the nature of your son's—
our son's lineage.

As is proper,
on this very day,
I shall announce Mordred as my son, and heir.

You have been a boon to me
these past few years,
but I cannot look beyond
Your deceitful use of me.

Go to your son.
Tell him about his true parentage,
and his new position.

Then tell him goodbye,
for you must leave Camelot behind,
never to return."

With a stunned sadness
and a gleam in her eyes she says,
"As you wish,
My lord King."

VII

After Morgaina's departure,
my rebounding health abandons me,
sinking to even lower depths than before,
causing me to become bedridden.

I drift in and out of consciousness
while clinging to the hope of the grail
with visions swirling through my brain:

Tutored by Merlin about man's nature;
Sparring Lancelot at a tournament;
Guinevere wearing wedding white;
Morgaina's love and seduction;
Mordred hovering, keeping a vigil.

As I open my eyes,
a world weary knight,
unkempt with a long, matted beard,
tangled hair, and dirty grey skin,
kneels before me.

Is he real or a vision?
To determine which,
I reach out my hand,
and lay it upon his head,
"Who are you?
Are you a shade?"

"It is I, Sir Percival, my lord King.
I am real and returned from the quest.
I have achieved the holy grail!"

Quivering at his words,
I say a small prayer in thanks.

Percival reaches behind his back
Bringing forth a cup-shaped bundle
wrapped in an oiled cloth.

With a bowed head,
he opens the bundle,
revealing an earthenware cup.
"King Arthur,
I present the Chalice to you."

Angelic voices sing,
bouncing around my sickroom,
and echoing in my ears.

"Mordred,
fill this cup with my elderberry wine."

"Yes, my lord."

Percival leans forward,
bringing the cup to my lips,
tipping it towards my open mouth,
and allowing me to drink.

The liquid fills my throat,
runs down my chin,
and onto my bedclothes.

I feel a fire rising from my soul,
spreading over my body;
settling in my brain.

My eyes roll back to their whites,
and for a blinding instant,
I merge with Morgaina
("Arthur, I feel you.")
seeing myself.

Intertwined souls
of an eternal cosmic love
existing to strengthen,
and offer succor;
Two halves of a mystical force.

With a surprised understanding,
I cry out a throaty bellow,
"Forgive Me!"
And I feel her smile sweetly.

Awakening refreshed and revitalized,
the shroud of despair that surrounded
my soul and Camelot blows away;
The grail leaves us healed and pure.

VIII

Racked with guilt from the affair,
Guinevere hacked her hair short,
traded her finery for sackcloth,
and doused herself in ashes.

Walking to the outskirts of Londinium,
she begged admittance into
The Cloister of the Wounded Soul.

"Greetings King Arthur!
We welcome the honor
of your presence to our humble home."

"My pious Abbess,
I hope the afternoon finds you well.
I have come for an audience
with my wife, Guinevere."

"Yes, my lord.
I will inform Sister Gwen of your arrival."

Leaving me on the stoop,
she closes the door,
returning inside.

A few minutes elapse.
The door reopens
and she bids me to enter.

Walking through a series of low passages,
we arrive at a small cell.

The afternoon light streams
through a window set high in the wall,
coating the room in a pale gold.

Furnished in a rude fashion:
A roughly hewn bed against the wall
with a writing desk and a chair
underneath the window.

On the edge of her bed,
sitting near the center,
Guinevere faces towards me
with her hands folded in her lap,
gazing downward.

Lifting her head and looking at me,
I see traces of the girl I married.

"Hello Arthur,
You look well.

After all these years,
I am surprised to see you."

"When Sir Percival brought the grail to me,
a shroud tore from my eyes
and I decided to make amends.

May I sit?"

"Pray do."

Pulling the chair close
with our knees almost touching...

"I first saw you when we had won the day.
As I had slain the enemies lying at my feet,
you were a vision I wanted to conquer.

Your father's joke transformed my lust,
and I wanted to marry you.

Over the years my attention drifted
and I did not show you
the affection that you deserved,
driving you into Lancelot's arms.

I recently realized destiny tied
you and Lancelot together,
but I used my lust and position to interfere
with the natural progression.
(Taking her hands in mine…)
Will you absolve me of this burden?"

"My dearest Arthur,
The fault of what happened
between us cannot be so easily placed.

We both contributed to the cause,
and, no matter my feelings,
I broke my vows to you.
(Leaning in, she kisses my forehead…)
I free you from your guilt.

But I want you to do one thing for me:
Go to your brother-in-arms, Lancelot,
And release him from his penance;
Restore your bond of friendship."

"Yes, Guinevere!
I will go to him."

Bong! Bong! Bong!

"The bells for Vespers sound,
signaling the time of your departure
and my time for prayer."

Standing together,
I embrace her in a brotherly hug.

"Thank you for visiting,
my Lord King."

"Goodbye Guinevere,
my Queen."

IX

Unsure of how my arrival will be received,
I prepare a small retinue:
knights, men-at-arms, and infantry.

With my armor polished to a sheen,
Excalibur on my hip
and my banner,
a red dragon on a field of gold,
flapping in the wind,
I mount my white charger.

Preparing to leave forthwith,
I motion for Mordred.
"We are journeying to Brittany.
Remember my counsel,
keep your head about you;
Represent me while I am away."

"Yes, father."

Traveling at a steady trot
over the rolling countryside,
we cross the Channel,
and, in a matter of weeks,
arrive at Lancelot's castle.

With my men standing at the ready,
I dismount my horse
and cross the moat.

Walking over the open drawbridge,
the planks creak from my weight
as toads croak below me.

The empty courtyard,
A disheveled mess,
Blossoms with weeds and debris
as if abandoned in a rush.

Across from the main keep,
a small chapel peeks from the corner
with a crumbling wall toppling against it.

Sound bounces around the castle's interior,
echoing from the chapel.

Whoosh... Cra-CK!

My blood pumping,
I draw my sword and approach with care,
a heightened awareness surrounds me.

Whoosh... Cra-CK!

Set in a wrought iron pricket,
an old Easter candle radiates a gloomy light,
shining on a figure kneeling before the altar.

Whoosh... Cra-CK!

A whip whistles,
flying through the air,
biting into his exposed back.

Whoosh... Cra-CK!

"I am sorry!"

Whoosh... Cra-CK!

"My flesh betrayed me."

Whoosh... Cra-CK!

"Forgive me!"

"Lancelot!"

Whoosh... Cra-

Grabbing the whip out of the air,
I pull it from his hands.

"Lancelot!
I have come for you.
You may stop your punishment."

"A-Arthur?!
Not a wraith to torment me,
but in the living flesh?"

"As your equal and your friend,
I am here.

Come to me.
I offer you my forgiveness.
Let us bury our past transgressions
and reforge our friendship."

He staggers over,
falls to his knees,
and wraps his arms around my waist.

"Thank you!
O, Thank you!
I have waited so long for this day!"

"Stand up, man!
Join me!
Let us leave this desolation
and find a place to heal,
reliving our glory days."

X

Summer fades as Fall transitions,
and I receive word from home.

"Greetings, my Lord King,
I bear tidings from Camelot;
Dire news has befallen your kingdom."

"What have you heard, Sir Kay?"

"One of my loyal footmen
risked his life by sneaking out of the castle
to bring this news.

Mordred, using spells and magic,
convinced the nobles and commoners
that you died fighting Sir Lancelot;
killed in the heat of battle.

As your only surviving heir,
those ready for a regime change
have thrown Mordred their support,
and forced the bishop to crown him king.

A contingent of your supporters
rebel at Camlann;
Mordred prepares a force
to march and crush them."

"Tonight, we break camp
and ride to face the traitors!
We must protect the legacy of Camelot."

XI

A rolling mist settles over the moor
as the sinking sun bleeds into the horizon
with a red-orange glow.
Hell's fire burns across the sky.

My son frantically looks around,
attempting to rally his troops
for a final assault.

Over the din of battle.
"MORDRED!"

The field falls silent.
All attention focuses
on the coming passion play.

"Embrace me for a final time."

"As you wish, father."

With a guttural roar,
he charges at me,
his hands wrapping a spear's shaft.

Planting my feet, I brace for impact.

As his body smashes into mine,
I am driven backwards.
The spearhead pierces my belly
traveling through my guts,
and explodes out my back.

By sheer force of will,
I stay on my feet.

Using my left hand,
I drag my body forward,
inch by agonizing inch,
traveling up the shaft
with Excalibur held ready.

Fixing him in place with my eyes,
I wrap both hands around my sword
and drive the blade into his chest,
pushing it straight through.
Blood bursts from his mouth,
splattering over my face.

Removing Excalibur with a yank,
its human sheath falls to the earth.

"It is over."

As I sink to my knees,
my mind drifts into oblivion.
Touching the fringes of the universe,
I pass out on the ground.

> *Having spent a week*
> *at the township of Camlann,*
> *meeting with my fellow solicitors*
> *and lecturing on the rule of law,*
> *I leave the King's End at closing time.*

Walking down an alleyway,
trying to find a cut through,
a group of blighters appear,
blocking my way.

"Gud ev'nin' Gov'n'er,
you need to pay the passage tax
an' we'll let you thru."

Not wanting any trouble,
I turn to retrace my steps
only to find the way blocked.

Left with no other option
I hold my walking stick by its shaft,
twist the handle,
and
click!
A hidden sword unlocks.

Twirling with a flourish,
I strike the leader first,
running him through with my rapier.

He collapses to the pavement,
and his shocked compatriots
rush me from all sides.

In a flurry of fists and clubs,
my arm goes numb from a nerve hit
and I drop my sword.

With a strike to the back of my head,
I sink to my knees.
In the moon, I see Lola watching.

Rough work boots trample my body
until everything goes black
and I pass out on the ground.

Splish,
      Splash,
            Splish.

Floating on a comfortable motion,
the waves break over the hull.
      A fog horn sounds in the distance.
I awaken with my senses open,
pain pulsating over my body.

I turn my head to the right.
A woman sits on the deck with folded legs,
my hand enclosed in hers.

"Morgaina?"
    "Lola?"

"Yes. I am here, Arthur.
    "Yes. I am here, Art.

I have you and you are safe.
    You have completed your journey.

We travel to Avalon.
    We travel to Avalon.

Where I will heal you for eternity."
    Where we fulfill the will of the Elders."

X. *The Book of Morgaina*

Browsing through my library,
gazing at the titles,
I amble among the stacks;
I want my attention grabbed.

A ribbed spine,
clothed in hand-worked leather
draws me towards it.

Gilded gold letters
embossed into a maroon skin
proclaim the title:
"The Book of Morgaina."

Grabbing the top corner,
I pull the book from its row.
Hidden wisdom radiates,
almost vibrating in my hand.

I tug the silk bookmark,
and, with a creak,
the pages open to the middle section.

The smooth vellum,
colored like an aged cream,
illuminates with marginalia:
A knight rides a rabbit, jousting a snail,
Kittens hang on a mushroom,
Snakes in a tree guard treasure.

I trace the letters:
Hidden scars left by a scribes' stylus
reveal themselves like braille.

Sliding a finger between the thick pages,
I flip to the book's beginning,
ready to rediscover my history.

I

Like Lilith before me,
an outcast and survivor,
I am connected to the earth—
My progeny destined to expand.

Having lived as a maiden and a mother,
I began to fulfill the third aspect
and feel comfortable in its power.

A decade after Arthur's demise,
with Camelot in ruins,
the world fell into chaos
as warlords ravaged the land.

During this time of darkness,
I founded the coven;
A place to guard the lore
and secret knowledge
of the ancient ones.

On a crisp, clear evening,
with a three-quarter moon lighting my way,
I travel upon a lessor Roman road.

Guiding my pony cart at a steady gait,
I feel the call of the Goddess
and the pull of the future.

I cross a small stream
and my wheels become mired
in a wash out created by a past torrent.

Planning to ride for assistance,
I unhook Ned from his cart.

Voices bounce over the air.
I peer through a wall of prickly shrubs
searching for the source.

Marauders divide their spoils,
discussing their planned destruction of Avalon.

I cannot allow this to happen!

Opening my third eye,
I converse with my inner self
and discover the best course of action.

Out of the deep ether,
I thread together a spell
fused with dark Magick.

This intricate mental tapestry
requires a price to be paid;
a sacrifice of some sort.
All I have to offer is my body.

Breathing three quick breaths,
I fill my brain with oxygen
and jump through the hedge.

Their surprise crests before me
and I ride it into their camp.

Striving to appear manic,
I throw my arms in the air
and wave my staff frantically.

"Beasts that pass for men,
Hear me speak!

I am Morgaina of the Fey,
Keeper of the Goddess,
Subjector of Warriors,
Destroyer of Camelot.

I know your plans.
I have heard of your conquests.
I am here to prevent you
from inflicting further suffering."

"Ha!
What can you do old woman?"

Pointing my staff at the moon, I call out:
"Infundere me cum potentia!"
(Infuse me with power!)

As it permeates the wood's grain,
an angelic beam streaks across the sky,
pulsating my body with its energy.

I mumble a small prayer
and swing my staff.

The force of the Goddess
explodes the chieftain's head
in a muffled wetness
and he crumples in a heap.

After a shocked pause,
the remaining men overcome their astonishment
and swarm like locusts,
their boots, fists, and clubs pummeling.

A gloved fist expands in my vision,
shattering my face.
I collapse to the ground,
avoiding the fire by mere inches.

In a state of suspended consciousness,
I am lifted and thrown about,
only aware of the spell held in my mind.

Warm liquid splashes over my head,
reviving me into the moment.
Dripping down my face,
over my parched, swollen lips,
I taste salty urine on my tongue,
burning as it soaks.

"Look!
The witch awakens!
Let us teach her about conquest!"

My arm sockets unhinge
as I dangle between two trees.
My knees drag on the ground.

Handling me like a rag doll,
they rip and tear my clothing.
Naked as raw beef,
I shiver in the chill night air.

A presence moves behind me,
grabs my hips in both hands,
and lifts me to my feet.

A force at the center of my back
pushes me forward,
bending me at my waist.

The ropes tighten on my arms
and blood rushes to my head.

There's a rough fumbling between my legs.
"She's dry as dust.
Get her ready!"

Glutinous spittle splatters over my bottom,
slathered into my lower orifices.

As hard molten flesh invades,
tearing me apart internally,
blood flows down my legs.

Detaching my mind,
I float away from their harm
and continue to reinforce my spell.

Bringing my eyes into focus,
a horned beast stands before me,
holding his cock in my face.
He tries to force its head into my mouth.

I see him talking at me,
but cannot hear his words.
Leaving my place of safety,
I open my ears.

"Come on!
Open your mouth!"

I tighten my lips
and shake my head,
moving with a negative motion.

"Open your mouth!
You old crone!"

Again, I nod no.

He creates a pair of fists
and drives them into my head,
punching my eyes, cheeks, and ears.

Forming the last part of my spell,
I give up and do as he wishes.

He shoves himself down my throat,
gyrating in a pumping rhythm,
his belly smashing my ruined face.

As he abuses my mouth,
I open as wide as I can,
whistling a deep breath
through my broken nose.

Clicking my teeth together,
I bite down as hard as possible,
slicing through his member.
His pleasurable moans
transform into agonizing howls.

Spitting his sausage onto the ground
with his blood pulsating over my face,
I release the spell.

"Dea Auallonia defendat et salvum me!"
(Goddess protect Avalon and save me!)

Divine power floods through my being.

Pulling my arms together
and flexing my muscles,
my bonds explode to dust.

The air rushes away with a hiss
And a ball of light implodes
(THWOOM!)
expanding outwards,
vaporizing my attackers.

Looking around, I stand alone,
surrounded by man-shaped piles of ash
scattering on the soft breeze.

Feeling light-headed from my ordeal,
I stumble, nearly collapsing.
A warm nose nuzzles my hand...
Ned has come to steady me.

Using my last ounce of strength,
I climb on his back
and whisper,
"Home."

In a state of suspended consciousness,
I hear a rumble of questions and concern.
I feel the cradle of safety
in the cool comfort of fresh sheets.

II

After my defilement,
I awake but cannot see.
Everything is black,
with my body swollen
and radiating pain.

To escape the present,
my thoughts drift back to my beginnings.

Born on the vernal equinox,
with the moon's mark on my shoulder,
I have always felt at one with the Goddess.

My mother, a daughter of royalty,
held a place of honor
as handmaiden to Queen Ygraine.

Related through a distant ancestor,
they favored one another
like a reflection in a pool.

The yammering gossip of castle life
led me to believe my father was a man
of great power— possibly a wizard.

As I lay in my mother's arms,
listening to her sleep,
a great cacophony erupts
through the lower levels,
echoing up an adjoining stairway.

Ever the curious one,
I roll out from her embrace
and wander to the doorway.

Looking down the hall,
I try to catch a glimpse.

King Gorlois returns from battle,
trailing muck and mud on the runner
as he hurries down the passage.

His features, face and body,
shimmer in a magical haze.
Someone else flickers below his skin.

Since I am beneath his notice,
basically invisible,
I follow him as he pushes his way
into the queen's chamber.

Peeking through the open door,
I see a smile spread on her face
as she recognizes her husband
through a veil of sleepiness.

Grabbing hold of the comforter,
he rips it off her
and tosses it to the floor,
leaving her exposed
and shivering in her nightgown.

The king crawls over her,
bunching her gown to her waist
and yanks her bloomers off,
throwing them over his shoulder.

Untying his britches,
he whips out his fleshy sword
and pounces on the Queen.

I sit cross-legged on the floor
watching as the scene plays out.

After overcoming her surprise,
she welcomes his advances,
allowing her body to flow with his rhythm.

Although she does not see it,
her husband's black hair and beard
continues to glimmer and shift,
revealing a clean shaven cheek
and sandy blond hair.

With an orgasmic grunt,
he shoves his hips
and collapses on top of her,
breathing heavily.

Rolling off the bed
and tying his pants into place,
he finally sees me
as I stare with a serious gaze.

"I know you are not King Gorlois.
I can see your true self."

"You, child, must have the touch
and powerful sight to see through
the magic of Merlin."

The stranger shoos me away
"Go back to bed.
These matters do not concern you."
He exits the way he came.

Queen Ygraine self-consciously
pulls her nightgown back into place
and straightens her bedclothes.
Her eyes glaze over as if with a glamour.

As I process what I witnessed,
I go back to my mother's bed,
lie down, and close my eyes,
slipping into sleep.

III

"Pray excuse this interruption, Madam.

In the courtyard,
your husband's men-at-arms
carry his body from the field of battle."

Standing and leaving the breakfast table,
regal and stone faced,
Queen Ygraine takes hold of my mother's hand
and allows herself to be guided outside.

As a somber tension rises,
I trail behind them.

The morning sun shines brightly,
piercing the cold winter air;
The King's men stand in two columns
with their banners unfurled in the breeze.
His body lies covered on a cart.

"Tell me what happened."

"The enemy outflanked us.
King Gorlois fought valiantly
until he was pulled from his horse
and run through by multiple swords.

His last words,
'For the Queen's honor!'"

"Thank you for your courage,
and for bringing him home to me.
You shall be rewarded."

The men bow in respect
and stand awaiting orders.

Turning to my mother, she says:
"Morgause, take me to my room.
I feel weak and need to lie down."

As we walk down the passageway,
her small voice whispers as an echo:
"Late last night he came to my bed.
He seemed different, but he was with me.
I do not know how he is now dead."

My mother catches sight of me.
"Anna, I am taking the Queen
to her chamber and will sit with her.

Go to our room
and start your daily meditations."

"Yes, Mother."

IV

Running among the turrets,
playing Chase the Waif,
I glance through an arrow slot
and spy a grand retinue
appear at the woodland edge,
flying red banners with a golden dragon.

After the castle gates open,
the drawbridge spans the moat,
and the party enters the courtyard.

The leader, with a crown on his helmet,
dismounts and announces himself
as Uther Pendragon, the high King.

Sneaking from the top of the wall,
I position myself in the shadows.
Peeking out, I absorb his finery:

A crimson cloak lined with sable
flows from the shoulders of his armor.
Polished to a sheen,
the sun reflects and glints
as he paces, directing his men.

The legendary weapon, Caliburn,
swings in its scabbard from his hip.

As he traveled the Glade of Innocents,
a water nymph held aloft the sacred blade
from the depths of a glassy pond.

Born from the fire of the Chalice,
Merlin advised him to take the sword,
and, through it, unite the isle.

He turns towards my hiding place
and I catch a glimpse of his face:
Clean shaven with sandy blonde hair.

It is the stranger!
The man who came to the Queen's chamber!

V

As tapers burn on each column,
their oily light smoking to the rafters,
the banquet begins with little fanfare.

The Queen shares the dais with Uther,
her belly ripe like an apple after its bloom drops,
and he addresses the waiting nobles.

"This feast brings me back to the recent past:
Gorlois and I fought side by side
to quell the Saxon uprisings.
Then, we celebrated our victories.

After an imagined slight,
he spirited away this lovely creature,
here to the fortress Tintagel,
and proceeded to make war against me,
his liege lord.

As my men besieged his castle,
he made the ill-advised decision to charge
directly into the heart of my forces,
leaving Ygraine a pregnant widow.

I have come to offer my condolences,
and, in the spirit of healing,
I offer my hand in marriage.

Also, to further our relationship,
I declare her unborn child to be my heir!"

As I slink away from under the table,
returning to where I was told to stay,
the gathered subjects stamp their feet
and clap their hands in celebration.

VI

Ygraine screams a yell of painful triumph
as my mother catches the baby.

After removing the birth residue
and clearing his airways,
she blows into his face.
With a frenzied cry,
he breathes his first breath.

I feel my spirit reach out
and connect with him.
Our souls intertwine.
Completeness surrounds me.

Boom! Boom! Boom!

A gruff voice sounds.
"Open the door!"

As a maid pulls the handle,
Merlin pushes his way into the chamber.
The Queen demands to see her child.

"Do not give him to his mother!
He is mine by right of contract.

To gain his lust's desire,
I hid Uther with a cloaking spell.
He took Ygraine in the guise of Gorlois.

The issue of that union is my payment.
I will take the baby with me!"

In the midst of the commotion,
my mother calms the child,
gently rocking while humming a lullaby
and wraps him in swaddling.

As she hands over the newborn,
he gazes into her face
and absorbs her features.

VII

On the eve of my twelfth year,
a visitor arrives to sit with my mother.
As they speak in the study,
I read in the library.

"Your daughter's potential exceeds belief.
Her psyche bombards my brain.
The time has come to focus her energy."

The gentleman enters the room
and I glance up from my book.

Bending down,
he takes my hand
and brings it to his lips,
tickling me with his beard.

"Hello, Morgaina.
I am Merlin.

Your mother and I have known each for years.
She has told me much about you.

Have you ever noticed a special sense,
an ability to know things,
or a different way of seeing the world?"

I nod yes.

"I knew it!
You broadcast a signal,
and others, like me, can see it.
You are a beacon in the fog.

I will help you to harness your abilities
and prepare you for your destiny.

Do you understand?"

"Yes, Sir."

"Very well.
We will begin on the morrow."

As dawn crests over the horizon,
I follow Merlin to a nearby meadow.
The dew dampens the hem of my skirt
and a slight chill settles over me.

After counting off his paces,
he uses his staff to measure the space
and flattens the grass into a circle.

"Here lies an intersection of ley lines.
The Dragon line flows from the north
and the Raven line from the east.
They encompass the earth's power.

Sit in the center
and close your eyes.

Let your breathing become steady.
Let go of all your thoughts,
Let go of all your feelings.
Just let your inner fire burn.

Sink your fingers into the soil.
Feel the coolness of the dirt.
Feel the life it contains.
Feel the beginning of the infinite.

Reach out with your mind.
Reach into the air.
Reach into space.
Reach through time."

The smooth reverb of his voice
sinks into my brain, transporting me.
The world's aura seeps into my vision,
and I grab hold of the intangible.

A time of unrest grips the kingdom.
Uther sprawls dying in a pool of blood.
Caliburn lies in the dirt, forgotten.

His vassals have ended his rule.
The betrayal of Gorlois burns in their memories.

Ygraine's son plays at his foster parents.
He's happy and unaware of his linage.

I reach out towards him
'Arthur, come away from her!'
and bounce elsewhere.

Drifting towards a full moon
I fall through a skylight.

I hover over an altar
and witness the splattering of blood;
the lifting of a beating heart.

'Take it,
Possess it,
For it's always yours!'

A vortex opens
and I am pulled into London's heavy fog.

I hear the rap tap tapping
on my chamber door
and the taste of absinthe
burning over my tongue.

I intake a quick breath,
and our blood intermingles
as warm droplets drip
(Drip, drip, plop!)
into a crimson puddle.

I fly out the window
with the breaking of dawn
and float back to my present.
Merlin keeps a vigil over me.

A worm pushes out of the earth,
and crawls over my fingers.
The slimy coolness of its skin startles me
and I am dragged back into my body.

As my eyes open,
I lie on the meadow
with the noon sun radiating
a comforting warmth.

VIII

I find the cast away Caliburn
overgrown with weeds,
and half-buried in dirt.
Remnants of the nymph's power
guides me towards it.

Carefully retrieving it from its grave,
I trace my fingers over the elongated shape.

As leather rots from the hilt,
the pitted blade, marbled with rust,
radiates reflections of the Chalice.

With my quest completed,
I return to the Dragon Line Temple
for the Spring Equinox.

The pregnant moon streams
through the ceiling aperture,
pouring over an alabaster altar,
causing it to glimmer with an otherworldly light.

As I kneel in the tangible glow,
the folds of my samite robe
drape over my body,
and glisten like silver.

I hold the ruined sword flat
and raise it above my head.
The blade mirrors the Goddess.

"I call upon you to purify this blade.
Restore its power!
Remove the falsehood of men!
Rescue the spirit of my water sister."

A bright red line of agony
twists in my intestines,
ripping from my crotch to my brain,
tearing me in two.

The pain expands from my womb
and materializes before my eyes,
forming into a faceted gem,
a blood ruby.

Lunar light absorbs into the sword
and death's shade eclipses the moon,
turning the night into pitch,
blacking out the celestial orb.

Spinning in a circular orbit,
the bloody stone attaches
to Caliburn's pommel.
A ring of fire flashes,
and mystical runes etch the blade.
Take Me Up, Cast Me Away.

Excalibur is born.

As I wrap both hands around the cross piece,
I scream a lioness' roar,
and drive the sword into the altar;
The steel sounds a high pitch whine
while sparks shower over the slate.

With an exploding flash,
the sword in the stone disappears
and I faint away,
falling into a deep slumber.

As I sleep, I dream.
I dream of a bedraggled park
hidden behind a hedge
with a slight mound at the center,
guarded by creatures of legend.

Here, Excalibur waits in its sheath of rock,
waiting for the coming of the King,
waiting for Camelot.

My dream transforms into a vision,
a vision of my future;
A future where—

——

A wind gust blows through the window,
flipping the pages,
traveling over the years.

With a slap of my hand,
I catch the turbulence
and open to the final chapter.

———

XXIX

A rolling mist settles over the moor
as the sinking sun bleeds into the horizon
with a red-orange glow.
Hell's fire burns across the sky.

As the battle commences,
I sit on a granite hillock.
A father has come to rein in his son.

The clashing of arms echoes in my head
and spills blood that seeps into the earth,
its thirst never to be quenched.

Meditating in the lotus position,
my mind melds with the chief combatants.
Their personalities duel within me.

I mustn't fail my men.
I'm not worthy of their blood and loyalty.
I still don't believe his betrayal.

I need this victory.
How are they this strong?
Where's my father?

"MORDRED!"

The spear pierces my flesh
and plows through my belly.
My gut burns with agony.

In a loving embrace,
Excalibur drives into my chest.
Blood spurts from my mouth
as my muffled cries murmur.

Collapsing in a heap,
I lie on the ground dead and dying,
drifting in their pain.

I take a deep breath and clear my mind.
The time of my mourning has arrived...
I must go see to my son.

My followers help me to stand,
and I make my way to the moor.

The war-weary men,
confused and lost,
part before me like the Red Sea
as I pass through their crowded numbers.

My boy lies broken on the ground,
limp and papery white.
Falling to my knees,
I cradle him in my arms.

Squeezing like an anaconda,
I try to reconnect our telepathic cord
and force my life into him.

Blurry grief flows through me.
I look towards the sky
and bellow my sorrow
into the falling twilight.

My son is dead.
He is beyond my reach.

The whine of his spilled blood
drives a spike into my brain.
The great sword calls for my attention.

Removing the soiled Excalibur
from Arthur's loose grip,
I wipe off the remnants
of Mordred's essence.

Once embedded in stone
and held aloft as a unifying symbol,
now restored to my care;
An object of psychic power.

Bending down, I caress Arthur's cheek.
"Our lives have been intertwined.
I saw as you entered this world,
and I am here to guide you beyond it."

I motion to my men with a wave.
"The time has come to exit this field of death.
Make the King comfortable
and retrieve Mordred."

Brought to Avalon,
dying from his son's death stroke,
Arthur's placed on a pyre
to rejoin the universe,
He will return again
as the once and future King.

——

With wax dripping onto the floor,
the candle burns to its base.
I close the book and replace it on the self.

As the Winter Solstice draws near,
the time of our transfiguration approaches.
The will of the Elders comes to fruition.

XI.   *Winter Solstice*

Darkness floods around us,
heightening our fear.

Clutching your hand
and holding it tight,
we run to my chamber
to escape our fright.

Bolting the door
to keep the demons at bay,
I turn to you, kneel, and pray.

You are my beauty,
my gorgeous girl,
the mother of light,
and sister of the world.

Reaching out with trembling hands,
I pull you towards me
as if to make amends.

It's time to worship,
to awaken the night.
Let's enter the Goddess
and celebrate her light!

You pull your shift
up over your head
and expose your body
for our marriage bed.

I trace your curves
with the tips of my fingers,
feeling goosebumps rise
as your hair follicles linger.

The pitch of night
fills the room,
and your body glows
in the dark of the moon.

As I lean forward,
my tongue tastes your middle.
Sliding into your navel,
I make you giggle.

I take your nipple into my mouth
and it throbs to attention
as your heart beat transmits
our love's tension.

Stretching my body,
I stand to my full height.
I wrap my arms around you,
and hug you tight.

With a tilt of your head,
you look into my eyes.
Drowning in your golden pools,
I release my spirit as my body dies.

Struggling for life,
I need your essence.
Coupling our lips,
I absorb your presence.

Pushing you onto the bed,
I prepare for our rite:
The end of darkness
and the birth of light.

Stripping off my clothes,
I unsheathe my sword.
You are my scabbard
and the keeper of the Word.

The power is yours
as the Chalice of life.
I am your servant
and you are my wife.

On this darkest night,
I surrender to your pleasure.
I'm willing to sacrifice
to achieve everlasting treasure.

Climbing on the bed,
I hover over your skin.
Enjoying its landscape,
and thinking about sin.

I dive for your cup,
licking my lips
and drinking your magick
as you thrust your hips.

Your legs lock around me,
holding me in place.
I am mesmerized
as you ride my face.

Our bodies begin to merge,
and our spirits mingle.
Do not fight the forces,
we are not meant to be single.

My shaft pulsates,
hard and veiny.
I move to enter you,
driving you crazy.

Your warmth surrounds me,
tight and smooth.
With each thrust,
we ride to a groove.

Moans like music
glide from your mouth
as our bodies transcend
and float from the house.

Turning invisible,
we travel across the nation,
spreading our love
to each and every station.

We are transformed
into something new.
Bright and beautiful,
we glisten like dew.

We are transfigured,
becoming one.
Base metal to gold,
we have just begun.

Having served our purpose
of restoring the balance,
we fall back to earth
to begin our penance.

Because I love you,
I am not forlorn.
Darkness is over
and the light is reborn.

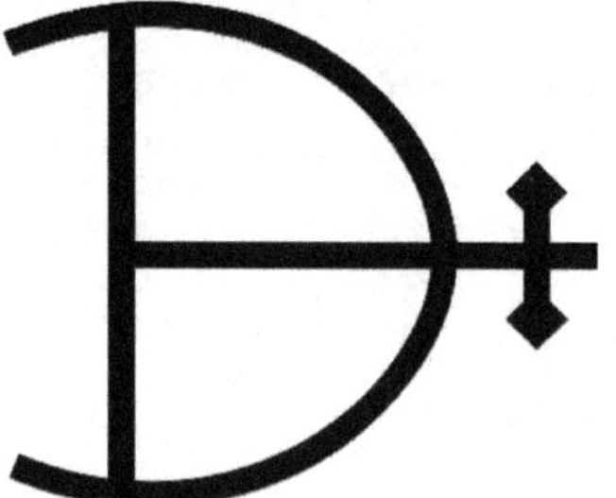

XII. *Love's Dawn (Reprise)*

-2013-

Having uprooted my life,
moving north from the islands,
I stay with a friend
as I try to get reestablished.

Feeling bored, lonely,
and slightly despondent,
I leave the apartment
to drive around town,
Searching.

Passing a newly opened club,
I feel a force draw me towards it,
and I guide my car into the lot.

After paying the cover,
I enter the main room
where I am led to a couch
overlooking the stage.

A vision of beauty materializes
and comes to me from the gloom.
Your aura reaches out
and I am enamored.

Piercing amber eyes,
bobbed ash-blonde hair,
luscious ruby lips,
firm body draped in the sun.

I feel a flash of recognition;
a familiar soul with new face.

"May I sit with you?"

"Yes, of course.
What's your name?"

"Call me Lola."

Our conversation ebbs and flows
as sweet nothings whisper between us.

With a demure glance, you ask,
"Would you like a dance?"

As I nod yes,
you take my hand
and lead me across the room.

Entering a dark alcove,
I sit on a bench
and wait for the music to begin.

You shed your dress
as your body moves with the rhythm.
I am entranced by your spell.

You are an agile angel;
a symphony of muscular grace.
With fluid magick, you embody the Goddess.

Our brief interlude ends
and we return to our seats.

As your drink nears empty, you say,
"I have to go to the member's lounge..."

Feeling a deep connection
and not wanting to lose you,
I have a flash of inspired hope.

"Can we go to the VIP area?"
A smile brightens your face.

Calling over an attendant,
we take a brief tour
and I pick a secluded room.

As the door closes,
we leave the noise
and club action behind.

With plush carpet and maroon walls,
the decadent splendor enfolds us.
The atmosphere tingles
as our essence mingles.

Your body flows over me,
like the ocean onto the shore,
teasing me with its sensual touch.

With a gentle forcefulness,
my lips are surprised
by the power of your kiss.

I have met my soul's fulfillment
and drown in your depths;
Our past connection renewed.

Like sand through my fingers,
time's minutes tick away,
and my night draws to an end.

As we stand near the bar,
I hold you in my arms.
Elation surrounds me.

With a final hug,
deep and all-encompassing,
we say our goodbyes,
and you whisper,
"My name is Anna."

Part II

Ripples from Dawn

I.   *Kissing*

With quickening heart beats,
our pulses race along.
I teasingly brush your lips with mine,
tasting you.

My arms around your back,
supporting your head.
Our lips purse together,
slightly parted.

Inhaling and exhaling each other,
we reach the apex.

Our lips separate
with a small light kiss.

II. *At This Moment*

At this moment,
everything is swirling around my head.
I see your gleaming honey-gold eyes as you look at me.
I see your smile and your lovely kissable lips.
I see your head twist away as you become shy.
I feel you in my arms as we stand stomach to stomach.
I feel your firmness as I hold you tight.
I feel your softness as I caress your hand.
I see your arm hair stand on end as you get goose bumps.
I feel your breath on my neck.

We need to explore us.
I want to make your body explode with pleasure.
I want to absorb your mind.
I want to hear about your life, passions, and dreams.
I am you and what I see is me.

III.   *Sunday Morning Musings*

Gazing at your sweet smile
through the mist of time,
I think of you.

The delicious curve of your lips
calls out for kissing.
Your bottom lip, a mound of joy.

Your skin tingles as I caress you,
sliding my fingers over your body,
feeling soft warmness.

When our gazes meet,
it is the sun rising over the ocean;
Golden over blue.

Your eyes are a window,
and their light draws me into you.

IV.   *The Passage of Time*

The passage of time
amplifies as it progresses.

Wonderful moments
grow into epics.

Feelings become less precise,
but more enveloping.

You are in my mind,
and I see you:

Your lithe body
as you move.

Your flowing hair
as it tickles my face.

Your luscious lips
as they caress mine.

Your glowing eyes
that reveal your soul.

————————————

Amplifying time is a thief;
It erodes as it goes.

Memories need to be refueled,
and refreshed:

New conversations
to expand our minds.

Ideas to fill in
and inspire.

The wonder
of
physical touch.

The burning of passion.

V. *Anticipation*

From across the room,
my heart beat increases.

Endorphins flood my blood,
I pursue happiness.

Sitting together in a comfortable clutch,
our hands intertwine.

Your hair plays across my lips,
I whisper in your ear.

Face to face we face one another,
your eyes in mine.

Leaning in,
space between us diminishes.

Tension rises,
Our lips hover.

Heat, pressure, and softness;
Our breath intermingles,
kissing ecstasy.

VI.   *A Backward Glance*

After too much champagne,
I lie on the floor,
trying to pull my head together.

You stand in the doorway watching,
supporting me with your words.

Everything in motion,
our evening is at a premature end.

Arrangements are made.
It's time to go.

I'm surrounded by security
and swept down the hall
into the early morning air.

"Go back inside.
You can't be out here dressed like that."

I glance backward
and behold you:

Standing on the stoop,
arms slightly crossed,
a despondent look on your face;
A picture of beauty.

At that moment,
I want to hold you,
to comfort you,
but there is no going back.

I have overindulged,
and am paying the price:
No final goodnight.
No caresses nor sweet whisperings.

VII. *The Present*

The past does not define,
but affects and we learn.
Our best hope is to live fully
without the taint of bad experiences.

The seeds of the future form as we live.
Let us court happiness
and cultivate it.

We follow our minds
and our hearts in equal measure.
But we must JUMP sometimes
and trust everything will be fine.

The golden ring is in sight
And it's yours to hold.

VIII. Thinking About You

My chest feels tight,
my breath is short,
and my heart is racing.

This is a heart attack—
But not the bad kind.

Holding you in my arms:
Contentment.

I said that you like me too,
and you ask, "How do you know?"

The way you look at me,
a sideways glance, and a shy giggle.

The way you hold my hand;
a firm confident grasp
as your fingers trace down my arm.

IX.   *Every Day*

Every day
I live my life:
Wake up.
Hang out at work.
Go home.
Eat dinner.
Go to bed.
Start over.

There is an emptiness that cannot be filled.
I am tired of being alone.

I see and meet people all of the time,
but it seems impossible to connect with the right person.

She has to be out there:

A beautiful, smart woman
who will fill in everything
I'm missing.

X. *Agile Angel*

Agile angel twirling through the air,
with hands grasping
and muscles tensing,
your body is fluid poesy.

Bright eyes,
ruby lips,
brilliant smile...
Your beauty mesmerizes.

Dancing brings joy,
dancing celebrates life,
dancing is passion
and it brings us together.

Everyone is watching,
but not everyone sees.
The art is in your heart,
and you are poetry in motion.

XI.   rorriM Mirror

Unknown desires fill my brain.
Outside, the world turns,
Yet everything stays the same.

Events gather like clouds,
Violent and dark.
Oblivion awaits unless
Life is fulfilling.

Individuals belong together:
I am yours, and you possess me.

Let our lives make
Oblivion dissipate.
Vision pierces the dark.
Everything is right and in sight.

Yet everything stays the same:
Outside, the world turns, but
Unknown desires are clear.

XII. *Ode to Dorian*

A cute little guy:
Coal black coat.

Perching on high,
sitting in baskets
under covers.

Glowing eyes are
always looking:
He protects his domain.

At dinner:
Ready to share
whatever Anna's eating.

Sitting in a sack:
His paw reaches out
for his mother's touch.

He is a forever kitten,
with a cute portrait
hidden away.

XIII. *Fantasy*

If we were lovers,
I'd trace your body with my tongue,
tasting your scent and sweat.

With a pull of your hair,
I bury my face in your neck,
testing your flesh with my teeth.

Moving my mouth over your breast,
my tongue flicks your erect nipple
and sucks its sweetness.

Your temperature rises:
Black panties are spotted white
into a shapely wetness.

Slowly peeling them away,
the cotton crotch sticks slightly,
revealing your nether lips.

Sliding up your inner thigh,
I tease with my tongue,
and you moan in anticipation.

As our lips meet in a kiss,
I part them with my tongue.
Your fluids flow in to my mouth.

With a rhythmic thrusting,
my tongue is a piston
in your fleshy channel.

Pulsating with your heart beat,
your swollen clit awaits
its orgasmic release.

Your breath sharpens
as pleasure ravages your body.

XIV. *Beginning Lovers*

As beginning lovers,
exploring one another;
we undress,
wanting our flesh exposed.

Showing restraint:
Each shirt button slowly releases,
deliberately increasing the tension.

Sensual hands touch skin
as soft caresses
create goose bumps.

A tongue traces a neck
across a shoulder blade,
around a belly button,
sucking tenderness.

Engorged flesh,
trapped in a cloth prison,
pulsates with a natural rhythm.

Releasing the prisoner
and removing the restraints,
flesh is revealed to flesh.

Erect and at attention,
I absorb your naked beauty;
the embodiment of perfection.

Pushing me on my back:
You stroke my mass
while fondling its head.

Dripping nectar,
you reposition yourself,
yin over yang.

With silky wetness,
your vulva envelops my cock,
sliding on my shaft.

In a teasing motion,
my head traces your labia.
It slightly gaps,
awaiting my thrust.

Your breast is in my mouth,
a flickering tongue plays on an erect nipple…
Your body releases pent-up emotion!

Satisfied:
In each other's arms,
we pass out with pleased exhaustion.

XV. *Lonely Man Fulfilled*

A lonely man:
Empty hearted,
looking to fill a need.

There are people that love him,
and he loves them too,
but it is not enough, not fulfilling.

He wants true love,
his other half,
but has given up the search.

One night, out at a club,
he met someone,
And things changed.

She is a rare combination:
An intelligent beauty,
an artist,
a writer.

Watching her dance:
Fluid beauty.

Her sculpted muscles tense and flow:
Breathtaking,
art made flesh.

Exploring her mind:
They have different ideas,
but compatible thoughts
and similar views.

When alone together:
Their bodies ebb and flow
as the ocean plunges on the shore,
bringing each other to sensual heights.

This wonderful woman:
Great joy and happiness.

XVI. *Halloween*

Goblins, ghouls, and ghosts...
Are they what scare us the most?
It's the time of year they come to play,
running around 'til the break of day.
Scary monsters and super creeps...
Don't let them hear a peep.
They will take you away,
Never to see the day.

Hold your loved ones tight
and pray for the light.
Death stalks at the door,
waiting for you to open it a little more.

This night comes once a year,
allowing you to embrace your fears.
After being scared
and living on the edge,
life will be keener,
sweeter,
and more intense.

Let us go out this night!
Let us be afraid and scared!
Let us hold each other tight!
Let our lives be amplified!

XVII. *Possible Reality*

We met in a place of fantasy.
Is reality a possibility?

When we are together,
everything fits.

Sitting in silence,
warm comfort.

Staring into your eyes,
I could lose myself.

Your sweet smile,
a slice of sunshine.

I love to hear about you:
Your life, opinions and experiences.

You inspire me, beyond myself,
to try new things.

I want to share with you,
and bring you into my world.

I cannot explain it,
but we are good for each other.

If given the chance,
we will enhance each the other's lives.

XVIII. *End of the Evening*

At the end of the evening,
our bodies press together,
with our lips embracing in a passionate caress.

Your muscular back is revealed
as I move the zipper down your spine
to your rounded bottom.

Your dress puddles to the floor
and my fingers slide along your shoulders,
down your arms,
to the tips of your hands,
trailing goose bumps with a feather touch.

You step out of your dress
and walk towards the couch,
wearing only a black thong and high heels.

Bending you over the couch,
my eager hands peal
your panties down
around to your knees.

I trace my tongue between your cheeks
from your tail bone to your sex,
dripping saliva and marking my progress.

Resting on my knees,
I bury my face between your legs
and vibrate your lips with my tongue,
eating and sucking.
Blood swells into your pulsing clit.

I follow your crack with my tongue
from nether lips over your anus,
licking my way up.

As my pants slip down,
throbbing heat radiates
from my revealed fleshy mass.

With one hand on your lower back,
I guide myself inside with the other.

Smooth rounded flesh on your inner thigh,
my cock searches for his home.
Your labia opens slightly,
eager in anticipation.

My head swirls around your lips,
and I tease you with the idea of penetration.

Taking you by the waist,
my hips move forward.
You gasp as my engorged head enters
with pulsing heat into your channel.

My cock travels your cunt
in a steady rhythm.

Breath rushes in and out
as you ride the snake.

Timed with each thrust,
your finger pushes your button.
Creamy liquid streams
down my shaft, coating my balls.

Your entire body becomes flush
as your flesh trembles,
radiating miniature explosions.

XIX. *First Date Imagining*

Standing on the porch,
nervous butterflies
flutter in my stomach.

After meeting months ago,
this is our first date,
the chance to show how I feel.

Extending a finger
from my sweaty palm,
I press the doorbell.

After an eternity of moments,
and a rattling of locks,
the door opens.

A black streak rushes through the opening.
Your cat decides he wants out,
and scurries to meet me.

After a quick game of cat corralling,
Dorian makes his way inside,
and we meet again for the first time.

Enveloping you in my arms,
we exchange a hug in greeting.

Intermingling smells fill my nose:
Violet, jasmine, and lavender.

At an arm's length,
I absorb your beauty:
Golden eyes behind black rims
and deep red lips forming a smile.

Our gazes touch for a moment,
then you shyly look away.

As I wait in the foyer,
you retrieve your purse,
and we leave for dinner.

Going out for sushi,
I open the door
and guide you in,
my hand at the small of your back.

Playing with the chopsticks,
we eat edamame
and sushi rolls.

Lost in conversation,
the evening becomes late night
and it's closing time.

During the drive home,
surrounded in a comfortable silence,
we clutch hands.

Holding you on the front porch,
I lean in,
and our lips brush together,
exchanging intermingled breath.

XX. *Driving to Find Dinner*

Driving to find dinner,
a smile spreads across my face
as thoughts of you rush into my brain.

Comfortable around each other,
our defenses lower,
and our vulnerable selves become exposed.

Your eyes are a mirror,
reflecting me
and showing the real you.

Your shy smile
shines like a light
with your eyes cast down.

Your body,
a living canvas,
and art in motion.

Since that first night,
I have felt a deep connection.

XXI. *Transfiguration*

Longing and desire
morph into physical truth.

Nimble fingers
dislodge buttons,
and clothing sheds like a tired skin.

Hungrily, we nip and bite flesh,
becoming the other's Eucharist.
A new religion arises:
Passion's heat, the catalyst.

Worship begins with a kiss:
Full lips press together
and breath transfers between us.

Unexpected realms are entered.
Emotion erupts through your body
and streams down your face.

Your words echo my sentiments:
"You are the one."

You are loved.
With true intentions,
I offer myself to you.

XXII. *Reflections*

Gliding across the room,
you are a fluid work of art,
a study in muscular motion.
You're beautiful in a way you will never know.

I close my eyes,
breathing in your perfume,
enjoying the fleeting embrace,
and trying to capture it forever.

The year is ending,
introductions are over.
A deeper understanding takes root.

A new year dawns,
and a relationship blossoms:
Two halves form a stronger whole.

An unexplainable connection
that words cannot define,
but the stars hold the answer.

Lips brushing lips,
tongues tasting each other.
A hand runs along your thigh:
Small heaven.

Caught between desire
and a higher enlightenment,
we strive for Alchemy.

Animal feelings and passions burn hot,
transforming into life-sustaining gold,
spiritual ecstasy.

Your hand in mine,
a reassuring firm comfort.

An ocean in the sun's golden light,
our essences ebb and flow
as we gaze into the other's eyes.

Water and fire.
Signs of earth.
Air exchanged through a kiss:
We embody the elements...
Magick's beginnings.

We mold our minds with knowledge
and our bodies with weights.
We can remold our spirits
to their former shape:
Two souls merge into one.

XXIII. *Trust*

Enter freely
and give up everything.
Control is gone.
Your will is not you own.
Do not be afraid
for Love surrounds you.

As perfumed candles flicker
in a darkened chamber,
shadows play across the walls.
I grasp your hand
and lead you into our room.

Crossing the threshold,
anticipation shivers through your body.

Surrounding you in my arms,
our breathing syncs
and our senses sharpen in a decadent hug.

Excitement flickers around your tongue,
and my lips brush yours in a chaste kiss.

Dilated golden orbs gaze into mine
as the blind is tied into place.

Other senses quicken to compensate:
Touch magnifies,
Hearing becomes acute,
Taste and smell intensify.

With deliberate hands
and a flick of nimble fingers,
each blouse button pops open.

Navigating the newly formed crevice,
I slide my hands in,
exploring over the flesh of your stomach,
and push the shirt over your shoulders
until it's drifting down to the floor.

Taking you in my arms,
I reach the back of your skirt.

As the zipper slides down,
our parted lips meet.
Each click of its teeth is punctuated
with a flick of our tongues.

A small moan escapes you
as your skirt puddles to the floor.

Standing open and exposed,
I whisper in your ear:
"I am in Love and I am devoted.
I dedicate myself to you."

Black lacy bra with matching panties
and stilettos with bejeweled ankle straps...
Pleasure and release awaits.

I take your hand in mine.
We traverse the room,
and I sit you down on the edge of the bed.

Genuflecting before you,
I free your feet from their adornment,
untangling each ankle from its bondage.

My thumbs rotate over your sole,
massaging and caressing,
using all my fingers,
From your heel to each toe,
pressure points are enacted
and your entire body relaxes.

As you lie on your back,
my hands glide up your calves,
and alight on your knees.

With a slight force, I spread your legs apart
and reveal your inner temple
covered by the veil of your panties.

Using my tongue,
I travel between your legs,
kissing and tasting your thighs,
journeying to my church.

Reaching with my fingers,
I rend your veil.

As I suck on your lips,
exploring with my tongue,
your clit engorges from attention.

My finger slides inside,
then another.
Warm velvety smoothness
pulsates heat with each thrust.

As you grind on my face,
your juices flow over my chin.
The nectar of the gods.

With mind numbing pleasure,
a climax trembles through your body,
offering your energy to the Goddess.

XXIV. *Quiet Moment*

Sitting together
cuddling on the couch,
your head nestles on my shoulder,
and my arm wraps around you.

Holding hands,
our fingers intertwine.

Silence surrounds us,
there's no need for words.

We breathe together,
our hearts beating in tandem,
slow and steady,
and listen to the universal music
flowing through us.

We bring comfort to each other,
and find hidden strength.

XXV. *The Portrait*

In the museum of my mind,
hanging in a place of honor,
you are the portrait of Love
Incased in a gilded frame.

Special lights
suspended from the ceiling
brighten your features
and your beautiful hues.

Precious, rare, and life-sustaining.

A velvet rope
around the perimeter
keeps visitors at bay.

Sometimes,
when the guard is away,
I hurdle the barrier
To gain a closer look.

Using tactile senses,
I trace the curves of your face
and your golden eyes,
feeling the built-up layers—
oil paint upon oil paint.

You are art in its purest form.

With a refilled heart,
I exit the museum.

Leaving through the gift shop,
I purchase the portrait on a postcard
and put it in my pocket
to keep Love near me.

XXVI. *Muse Musings*

You are love and happiness,
and the world is better for it.
Although you are far away,
it delights me to know that we are friends.
I look forward to seeing you again,
catching a glimpse of your eyes,
and holding your hand.
Until that time comes,
I hope you are engulfed in perpetual joy.

XXVII. *Soft Flame*

You are a soft flame
burning inside me,
filling my heart
with a pure blue heat.

Once I tried to extinguish the flame
and bury it deep inside,
smothering it with forgetfulness,
but still, the flame smoldered.

Your kisses stoked the fire alive:
Burning bright,
beautiful,
and at full force.

I embrace the flame,
Its heat singes my flesh,
bringing happiness as it burns.

XXVIII.   *In the Temple of Aphrodite*

Well met in the temple of Aphrodite.
I drink glistening honey from your skin.
As you smother me with your body,
my teeth firmly bite your taut neck,
leaving my mark upon you.

Weaving my fingers through your hair,
I pull your head back
as a small moan issues from your throat.

Your full lips in front of my mouth,
I trace their opening with my tongue,
piercing the crevice.

Our tongues dance in a swirl of saliva
and our lips swell in a rush of blood.

With a slight squeeze, I cup your breast,
nipple standing hard in my fingers.
As I massage, knead, and stroke,
pleasure erupts from your chest
to your brain and through your body,
like a wave caressing the shore
causing your lips to tremble.

Pushing me to the floor,
you sit on the edge of the sofa with parted legs,
beckoning me to travel up your carnal highway
and satisfy my thirst at your chalice.

Crawling towards you,
I move my hands up over your knees,
journeying to your toned thighs,
squeezing them in a firm grip,
feeling you shiver in anticipation.

As I take you in my mouth,
your bud opens.
My tongue works its way inside,
twirling in clockwise circles.
Pressing your velvety nub,
I insert a finger with a rhythmic thrust
and sup at the sweet ambrosia
dripping down my chin.

Your hands guide my head
and keep my face in place
as you grind, sigh, and groan.
Moving to your knees,
you pull me up to my feet.

With nimble hands
and a fluid flick of your wrist,
you free my belt from its servitude,
popping the button of my pants.

As the zipper slides down,
tension pushes against the fabric
from the engorged flesh beneath.

With quickening breath,
you slip both hands into my waistband,
pushing my garments to the floor,
leaving me exposed in the air.

Grabbing my hips in your hands,
you pull me forwards,
and with a liquid grace,
you take my cock into your mouth:
Sensually kissing my helmet,
wrapping your lips around.

Exploring my shaft with your tongue,
your head bobs like a floating cork.
With a gagging effort
and watering amber eyes,
you swallow me down your throat,
my jewels resting on your chin.

Choking as you disengage,
you attack with a furor,
bringing me to the edge of oblivion.

With a final swirl and lick of your tongue,
you pull away slowly.
A viscous liquid suspends in the air,
trailing from the tip of my staff
to your lower lip's mound,
glistening like a rainbow.

Bending down,
I take your chin in my hand,
angling your lips towards mine
and explore them in a full-bodied kiss,
tasting the remnants of my musk.

Removing the rest of my clothes
I slide next to you.
Our naked bodies melt together.

Big spoon surrounding the little one,
I enter you from behind.
Your tight heat burns my core.

Wrapping a hand around your throat
and the other over your mons pubis,
I squeeze and press in time with my thrusts,
heightening your pleasure.

Moving to the missionary position,
our bodies crest on the waves of passion,
your hands clawing my back.

As the wave breaks,
your eyes roll
and your body quakes,
exploding in an orgasmic epiphany.

Your body begins to relax,
and, at the last moment, I pull out,
straddle your head,
and shove my member into your mouth.

As you drink my milk,
you suck me dry,
swallowing my vitality.

With a weakened body I lay back on the sofa,
wrapping you in my arms.
Our naked bodies flow together,
transferring heat,
resting as one.

As we drift off,
floating on a cloud of contentment,
I notice a cum droplet perched on your lip.
Closing my eyes, I take it into my mouth
and give you a soul kiss,
transferring the last of myself into you.

XXIX. *Universal Force*

There is a force flowing through the universe,
bouncing off the planets,
and whispering through the stars.

Close your eyes,
clear your mind,
and listen.

Do you feel it?

A pulse,
a backbeat,
a soft hum,
vibrating at the base of your skull.

It's magnetic,
drawing us together
and bringing me into obit
as one of your moons.

As gravity pulls,
swinging me around,
your beauty radiates from the surface,
inspiring me.

Through written word,
I try to inhabit your brain,
reflecting what I absorb.

Channeling thoughts and feelings,
I want to affect you,
hoping to give back what I receive.

You bring me joy and happiness,
and I love you for it.

I no longer try to understand.
I just accept and bask in your light,
feeling the universal force.

XXX. *On Beauty and Happiness*

My beautiful Goddess,
I am filled with Love
and regard for you.

You are the daughter
of Athena and Aphrodite;
my muse on Earth.

Seeing you
recharges a receptacle
of joy in my mind.

Our time together,
fleeting,
but I cherish every second.

When I leave you,
I want our embrace
to stretch into eternity.

You carry my heart
In your pocket.
It is yours to do with as you please.

Ghosts of you reveal themselves in others,
but they are only a pale vision,
as they lack your spirit.

In my mind's eye,
we will live life together
supporting one another's dreams.

I want you to be free from pain.
I want you to be free from strife.
I want you to feel Love in your heart.
I want you to feel surrounded by Love!

I want you...

XXXI. *Dream of Kissing*

Floating in a dream,
I take both your hands in mine,
pulling your body close.

As I wrap you in my arms,
giving a tight hug,
your muscles are a delicious firmness.

With a splayed hand,
I slide my fingers through your hair,
pushing it behind your ear.

Nibbling at your lobe,
I inhale a hidden perfume,
like fresh lilac.

A swirl of electric energy
dances in my brain.
A spark arcs between our poles.

As your lips beckon me,
I lean in with a parted mouth,
eager to taste your sweetness.

Lips almost touching,
I breathe in your breath,
my anticipation rising.

Soft lips join
as our tongues intermingle,
Joy erupts as...

Errrrn!
Errrrn!!
Errrrn!!!

A shrill sound rings in my ears,
bursting my dream
and ending my respite from reality:
The morning alarm awakens me.

You are miles away...
I miss your touch,
your voice,
and dream of kissing you.

XXXII.   *A Life Together*

Would you like to build a life together?
A life of supporting one another.
A life of companionship.
A life that grows our dreams.
A life devoted to happiness.
A life exploring our desires.
A life lived to the edge of ecstasy.
A life of passion.
A life of love.
A life of low moments and quiet solitude.
A life of deep kisses and holding hands.
A life exploring literature.
A life of a muse and her poet.

XXXIII. *Objectification*

You are not an object.
You embody beauty.
You exude love.
You possess wisdom.
You are the abstract made flesh.

You are my reality
and inspire inspiration.

I tremble to be near you.

Sitting together,
absorbing one another,
we live through quiet moments.

Communicating through touch,
my fingers trace patterns on your palm,
reading our future together.

Kiss me.
Kiss me softly.
Bite my lip
and kiss me again.

Twisted bodies
lay tangled together,
Your breathing,
a satisfied whisper.

XXXIV. *As I Think About Love*

As I think about love,
my thoughts drift to you.

I feel your aura,
and the happiness you bring.

The fleeting time we spent together
feeds my creative soul.

I long to see you,
and to hear your voice.

My memories sustain me
while I wait for you.

XXXV.   *A Quiet Evening*

Outside the window,
the last strands
of the setting sun
streak the sky.

You lie on the sofa
using my lap as a pillow.
A black ball of fluff
nestles at the bend
of your knees.

Holding a leather-bound book,
gilded pages hand sewn into the spine,
I use a ribbon marker
to open where we left off.

Exploring the metaphysical poets,
I follow the cadence of their words,
the rhythm of my voice vibrating.

Closing your eyes,
images appear
and float in your imagination.

I caress your hair with my free hand
and trace the edge of your jaw
with a gentle stroke.

As the past speaks in the present,
I absorb the unspoken poetry
flowing between us.

These small moments
give meaning to life.

XXXVI. *An Afternoon Meeting*

I

In my office at work,
I receive a surprise:
a bouquet brimming with summer flowers...
Dahlias, Marigolds, and Peonies.

Flush with excitement,
I pick an envelope
out of the arrangement.

Lifting the edge with my nail,
and sliding my finger across,
I rip open the glued flap.

My receptionist watches
as I tug the card
from its snug enclosure.

On a linen paper rectangle,
flowing cursive
written in midnight blue black
with a fountain pen's nib:

Meet me on the fifth floor,
Suite 507 at 2:30.
I want to be inside you.
 *A*

My cheeks glow rose
as a blush burns
its way across my face,
and my body reacts
with a rush of wetness.

As I become turned on,
my skin grows hypersensitive.
Fabric rubs against my hair follicles
and sends shivers down my spine.

Beneath my bra,
my nipples engorge,
pushing into their silk enclosure.

A little embarrassed,
I casually replace the card
and try to act naturally
in front of my employee.

Glancing at the clock,
It's only 11:30!
I have three hours to wait.
Hopefully I can focus
on my appointments until then.

II

At 2:15,
I head to the lobby
and press the elevator call button
with my index finger.

I watch the digital readout
countdown the floors:
6
5
4
3
And with a mechanical swish,
the doors slide open.

As my hand trembles in a nervous waver,
I aim for the fifth floor button
and mistakenly press the sixth.

Swallowing a deep breath,
my hand steadies and I try again:
With a precise click,
the button depresses
and closes the doors.

The elevator rattles up,
defying gravity,
and the doors open to the fifth floor.

Stepping out,
a plaque on the wall
gives direction:
500 - 510
--------->

Turning right and walking down the hall,
I mentally read off the door numbers.
My excitement builds:
500, 503, 504, 506.

507 comes into sight,
and my breath shortens.

Taped to the door,
a message in red marker
on a white poster board:

Please lock the door after you enter.
DO NOT turn on the lights.

Holding my breath, a little,
I grasp the knob,
turn it clockwise,
and enter the room,
thumbing the door lock behind me.

III

The office is empty
except for a large oak desk
sitting in the center.

A beautiful summer's day:
Afternoon light fills the room,
streaming in through mirrored windows
overlooking a local park.

From a dark corner,
Slightly behind me and to my left,
A disembodied voice issues a command,

"Walk to the desk,
Stand in front of it,
and face the park."

"Yes, master."

I enjoy this game.
I can relax
and relinquish control
while knowing I am safe.

Walking slowly forward,
I make sure my hips sway
as my heels click on the floor.
I feel his eyes touching my body,
watching every movement.

Stopping at the desk,
I await my next command.

"Get undressed.
Start with your blouse,
then your skirt,
your bra,
and, finally, your panties.

Keep your heels on
and pile everything on the floor behind you."

As a sultry jazzy riff plays in my head,
I unbutton the cuffs on each sleeve,
then pop the front buttons out of their holes,
letting my blouse slide down my arms
and billow to the floor behind me.

Reaching to my back,
I grasp the zipper of my skirt.

As my hips shimmy back and forth,
the teeth of the zipper click apart
until I drop my skirt to the floor
and kick it to rest with my blouse.

I unhook my bra,
the straps dangling from my arms.

"You are so beautiful,
I can't believe you are mine."
And I throw it to the pile of clothes.

Creating a show of removing my panties,
I grab the waist band in each hand,
and pull it tight over my hips,
accenting my butt with the elastic fabric.

Swishing my hips back and forth
and playing with the cloth,
I tug it in an exaggerated motion
and pull my panties down,
leaving them on the floor,
pushing my butt out as I bend over.

Standing straight again,
I await further instructions.
Through the mirrored window,
I watch the trees in the park
sway in the silent breeze.

I sense movement behind me
and the soft pad of bare feet.
I tingle in anticipation.

I hear smooth even breathing behind me
and his hands lay on my shoulders.

A smooth roughness on my skin,
I feel their potential strength
through his gentle touch.

His hands come together
tracing my shoulders
with the tips of his fingers
to the base of my neck.

With a slight pressure,
he follows my spine
to my buttocks
and grabs both cheeks
with a hungry grip.

I feel him lean forward,
and kiss my neck where it meets my shoulder.

A fire of electricity
erupts from my skin's nerve endings,
transmitting through my system
and escaping my lips as a low moan.

His lips glance my lobe while whispering,
"Can you bring your hands together
behind your back?"

I hear the whoosh of a silken cord
as he binds my wrists together.
The extra length dangles down
tickling the back of my legs as it sways.

"Turn around.
Let me see your face."

Doing as I'm told,
I twirl around
and look him over.

My downcast eyes
travel from his feet,
up his torso,
until I'm looking up into his face.

He stands naked before me
with the light from the windows
shining on his tall lean frame.
The trees reflect in the sky of his blue eyes
as his erection bridges the gap between us.

Taking my head in his hands,
he bends forward
and kisses me.

I part my lips wanting to take in his breath.
Our tongues dance in silvery streamers.

My body reacts to this stimulus:
My breasts become fuller,
my nipples harden,
and my womanhood aches.

Disengaging his mouth,
he whispers,
"Will you get on your knees?"

With lips numb from pleasure, I say,
"As you wish."

Helping me to the floor,
his cock throbs before my face:
A large purple head
and twisting ropy veins of his shaft.

My tongue licks his head
and I wrap my lips around the tip,
tasting the salty pre-cum as it flows.

Licking down his shaft,
blood pumps in the hardness.
I take his balls in my mouth,
Their musky scent fills my nose
and my taste buds.

As I shoot a pleading look,
"Master,
will you fuck my mouth?"
I leave it open,
awaiting his pleasure.

The head of his cock glides past my lips
and his shaft slides over my tongue
until it hits the back of my throat.

Holding my head in place,
he thrusts deeper,
his hips rocking back and fourth
with a heavy rhythm.

Breathing through my nose,
my eyes water as I fight my gag reflex.

Slowing his thrusts,
he withdraws his pulsing cock
and lifts me to my feet.

Lovingly wiping the saliva from my chin,
he gazes into my eyes and says,
"I am going to fuck you from behind."

I slowly nod my head in agreement,
words having left me.

He unties my wrists
and bends me over the desk;
I hold myself up with my hands.

He traces the expanse of my back,
down to my bottom.
Placing his hands between my legs,
he spreads them further apart.

His tongue parts my nether lips
as he drinks of my wetness.

A warmness begins to build up
and radiate from my stomach
to my nervous system.

Standing behind me,
I can feel him prospecting with his cock,
looking for the opening.

With my right hand,
I reach between my legs
and guide him inside me.

My lubrication flows
as his molten rod
travels my velvet hall.

I squeeze tighter,
gripping him
as he rhythmically pumps.
His cock grows harder.

Our flesh slaps together,
and he holds onto my hips,
driving deeper.

Pleasure builds through my body
as sounds and grunts escape my mouth
with only one thought in my brain:
fuck me!
Fuck Me!!
FUCK ME!!!

Everything becomes a blur,
speeding up,
and I am only aware of his cock
moving in my body.

With a tsunami intensity,
I explode in waves of pleasure,
and collapse on the desk,
no longer able to hold myself up.

From the rapid ferocity of his movements,
I can tell that he nears completion.
"I want...
cum inside me!"

With a final pounding stroke,
his balls slap my clit
and he fills me with a sticky saturating heat.

IV

Leaning against the desk,
breathing heavily,
he seems a little lost.

Reversing roles,
I take control.

Giving him a deep hug,
I absorb the sex smell from his body
and take his chin in my hand,
reaching up for a kiss.

"My darling,
Thank you for the flowers
and this surprise!
I had a wonderful afternoon.

I will see you later tonight."

Getting quickly dressed,
I kiss him goodbye
and walk out the door,
sending him a smile as I leave.

Entering my office in a hurry,
my receptionist gives me a knowing smirk.

"Please call my 4 o'clock.
Tell them that my afternoon meeting ran over,
and that I will be late."

As I walk to the back room,
I feel him dripping down my inner thigh
and I smile.

XXXVII. *Gazing from Afar*

I want to come over,
take you in my arms,
and kiss your beautiful mouth,
but, alas, that is not to be.

As in the knightly tales of old,
you are my Queen,
and I gaze at you from afar,
hoping for a token of your esteem.

Thoughts of you fill my mind,
and joy beats in my heart
as I await your return.

XXXVIII. *"I Love You"*

Close your eyes.
Imagine a world
where you are the center
of these simple words.

I want you to see me
as they whisper in your mind.

Do you feel them through your body?

Do they make a current flow
from your toes,
to your fingers,
to the tip of your nose?

In the middle of the night,
I wake next to you,
holding you tight.

Can you feel my breath on your neck?

Do you feel the heat of my skin?

You roll towards me,
and I kiss your pouty lips.

I love kissing you
and cannot hold back.

Words transcend language,
becoming enraptured,
capturing emotion.

Words have power;
I can touch you using my mind.

Words are magic,
and I give them to you:

I love you.

XXXIX. *Sometimes I am Afraid*

After a sensual, visual experience,
our essence intertwines,
and I have never felt us closer.

Holding you in my arms,
the heat of your being
melts into my flesh
and happiness saturates me.

With each kiss from your lush lips,
I seep further into your rapture,
losing myself but finding you.

You are my muse.

As a sacrifice on your altar,
I give myself:

Submitting to your desire,
basking in your beauty,
devouring your mind,
worshipping you.

You are central to my thoughts,
and linger forever
on the fringe of my soul.

But...

Sometimes I am afraid...
...That my heart will be broken.
...That someone else will become your world.
...That you will abandon me.

I work to overcome my fears
and live in perpetual hope.

I hope for a future with you.
I hope for your happiness.
I hope these threads weave together
as our life's intricate tapestry.

XL. *Whispering*

As I whisper your name,
each syllable forms
and I taste the sound.
The letters melt on my tongue.

Your vibrant spirit flutters
through my veins and feeds my heart.
Thoughts of you distill into delight,
bringing comfort to my soul.

I transmit waves towards you,
flooding the universe,
imagining your happiness.

As I whisper your name,
I want you to feel happy and loved.

XLI. *Happiness*

Lying on your side,
you pull your legs to your chest
and give me a sidelong glance.

I move beside you
and take you in my arms,
wrapping myself around you—
Your warmth conforms to my body.

I take your hand in mine,
and weave our fingers together,
feeling your strength.

We meld and become one,
as our hearts beat together,
with our breathing in sync.

Content and comfortable,
this is heaven on earth;
I do not want to let it go.

XLII. *Morning Thoughts*

Kissing you is bliss.
I love your body in my arms.

Exploring with my tongue,
I taste every crevice.

I want to possess you
and devour your mind.

You are perfection!
I need you to encourage and push me.

Thank you for being my muse!
Thank you for being in my life!

To me, you are Love.

XLIII. *As I Lie in Bed*

As I lie in bed,
I think about you:

Your pouty lips,
flowing hair,
sensual neck,
and sun-ignited amber eyes.

Slowing undressing
I kick my clothes to the floor.

Lying naked on my sheets,
thoughts of you flow in my blood,
bringing hardness to my cock.

Elongated with a full throbbing head,
my fingers lightly trace my erection
and play with my balls.

Your fire burns inside me.

With your scent filling my nose,
I can taste the strength of your tongue
as it shoves in my mouth.

Forming my hand into your pussy,
I move it rhythmically up and down my shaft.

I feel your tight wetness envelop me,
a liquid heat fueling my desire.

With my mouth on your breast,
I suck your nipple.
Its erectness is intoxicating.

I stroke at a faster rate,
my cock like steel.
Pre-cum leaks from the tip.

I kiss your mouth
as my hips pump faster.
Our flesh slaps together.

Your neck and face becomes flush,
and I feel your pussy clench my cock;
We are joined together for eternity.

You scream my name as pleasure explodes.
My stomach tightens and I find release
with glistening cum splattering on my belly.

Your essence surrounds me,
and I feel your closeness.

XLIV. Breathing Deep

Breathing deep,
I fill my lungs with oxygen
and a calmness spreads over me:
Thoughts of you fill my memory.

With your head tilted up,
you gaze into my eyes
and smile.

I push your hair over one ear,
and cup your face in my hand.

In a forward swoop,
I bend my mouth to your waiting lips,
breathing your breath as we connect in a kiss.

I feel absolute in your arms,
and eternity expands
during these fleeting moments.

As we disengage,
air particles fill the space between us,
and I feel a tether bind us together.

Watching you walk away,
I project my will to a future
where your electric touch
welcomes me again.

XLV. *Birthday Wish*

As a reward for surviving another year,
I can send a wish into the universe.

Surrounded by family and friends
singing the birthday song,
I sit in front of my cake,
the candles' light burning bright.

Slowing my breathing
and closing my eyes,
I lay my hands flat on the table.

Through my nose
I take a deep breath,
and fill my lungs,
My fondest wish floods my brain.

The song concludes
and I purse my lips,
pushing out the stowed air,
focusing the gust towards the light.

As the flames fight for life,
they flicker,
lose the battle,
and snuff out,
going dark with small coals left glowing;
A sacrifice towards my request's fulfillment.

Bold, Beautiful, and Brilliant;
I wish for ψου...

... το βε μψ βεστ φριενδ.
... το βε μψ ναυγητψ λοϖερ.
... το βε μψ λιφεσσ παρτνερ. *

*For wishes to come true
They must remain a secret,
and this one hides in a special font.

XLVI. *Submission Therapy*

Arriving twenty minutes early,
I learned to never keep you waiting.
I enter your sitting room,
nod to the receptionist,
and select a green, molded plastic chair.

Knowing me as a consistent client,
she marks my arrival in her day book
and speaks into her headset,
informing you I am on time.

Ten minutes after my scheduled appointment,
I hear the lock twist on your office door.

"She is ready for you, sir.
Please enter."

With darkness seeping around its edges,
I push the partially ajar door
and walk through as it swings open.

Illuminated under a spotlight,
a high backed mahogany throne waits
at the center of the room.

"Close the door."

Reaching behind me,
placing my hand on the knob,
I flip the lock as I shut the door.

"Remove your clothes.
Pile them at your feet."

Sliding out of my penny loafers,
I untangle my belt,
open my zipper,
and push down my pants,
followed by my briefs.

Loosening my tie,
I undo the knot,
drop it to the floor,
and unbutton my shirt,
freeing myself from its fabric.

As air conditioning fills the room,
goosebumps tighten on my skin,
and I await your further instructions.

"Walk to the throne and sit down."

Feeling exposed as I move forward,
the momentum and chilly air
causes my blood to flow,
turning me semi-erect.

Feeling embarrassed,
I use my hands as a shield,
trying to appear modest.

Lowering myself into the chair,
the well-worn mahogany caresses
my back and buttocks.
I prop my arms while resting my head.

"Open your mouth."

I comply.

"Wider."

From behind the chair
a pair of hands emerge
holding an electric blue ball gag.

The ball quickly installs into my mouth
as the black leather straps tighten,
fastening through the chair's back,
tying me in place and making me immobile.

Your heels click on the tile floor,
and you appear from behind me,
I shiver with anticipation of the unknown.

Your hair, like spun gold, flows
to the collar of a creamy silk blouse
with a hint of cleavage peeking through.

A black pencil skirt hugs your figure
as its hem meets matching stockings,
Red high heels highlight your feet.

"In today's session,
we explore your role as a submissive.
You do not have control.
Your will is not your own.
If you understand, nod your head."

I nod in the positive.

"You are in a safe and free place;
 I will subject you to a new experience.
Are you prepared to submit to my will?"

Again, I nod yes.

"We will begin with the familiar.
Spread your legs,
do not move your arms,
and stay still."

Kneeling before me,
you place your hands on my knees,
pushing my legs further apart.

Your upper body moves forward
as you drift into my lap.

I feel your tongue flick out,
And caress the tip of my flaccid penis.

You take me into your mouth,
blood rushes and hardness grows.
As my erection pounds the back of your throat,
your head bobs in time with your flowing body.

I moan around the ball
while trying to follow your orders.

You take all of me into your mouth
pushing your lips to the base of my shaft
and paint a lipstick ring.

Bringing me to the edge of oblivion,
you disengage,
leaving my cock throbbing blue
and glistening with spittle.

Using me for support,
you stand up,
walk to my ear and whisper,
"You will do that to me."

And then in a normal tone, you add,
"I am going to untie your gag.
You will sit here in silence
until I call for you."

The pressure of the ball increases
as the strap is freed from its buckle.
I push the gag from my mouth,
and watch it fall onto my lap.

As your heels walk away,
you turn off the spotlight,
and I sit waiting in the dark
with loneliness creeping in.

I hear you shuffle around the room:
The opening and closing of drawers,
the sound of your skirt's zipper,
the rustle of fabric as it is removed.

A soft light brightens behind me,
expanding like a new dawn,
and my chair's shadow casts
on the wall before me.

"I am ready for you.
You may come to me."

Standing and walking towards your voice,
I move around the throne
and towards the light.

Sitting on a purple satin sofa,
you have removed your blouse.
Your pink nipples stand hard,
signaling your interest.

High heels adorn your feet
with your thigh-high stockings
attached to a garter-belt.

Your skirt is thrown to the floor
and your legs spread like an eagle's wings.

In place of your panties,
you have inserted a fuchsia, strapless dildo.
It trembles as you flex your Kegel muscles.

Closing your legs
with the pink erection peeking out,
you lean forward
and motion for me to sit next to you,
patting the sofa with your hand.

Putting your arms around me,
and giving me a life-sustaining hug,
you pull me in for a kiss.

Our lips join together,
and I feel the texture of your tongue
as you taste my mouth.

You move my head to your breast
and shove your hard flesh into my mouth,
I drink from your nipple,
sucking and biting.

Breathing a breathless moan, you say,
"It is time for your next step.
Tell me.
What do you think will happen?"

Giving your nipple a final kiss,
I look down at your rubber hard-on,
and look into your eyes, smiling.

"That is correct."

You open your legs
and roll your waist forward,
pushing me to the floor.

With both hands around my head,
you lead me to your pink tower.

I open my mouth,
expand my throat,
and allow your member to enter.

I close my lips to create suction.
The smooth silicone hits my tonsils.
My eyes burn with tears
as I fight the urge to gag.

I hope my mistress appreciates my efforts.

Pulling breath in through my nose,
I exhale the shaft from my mouth,
and move to its base.

Your scent fills my nose and taste,
driving me wild.
I lick the edge of your nether lips,
savoring the tease of your pussy.

I try to remove the dildo
for greater access to your glory,
but you stay my hand.

"No.
You may not have that,
but I will fuck you."

Your right hand lovingly strokes your cock.
"Do you think it will fit in your ass?"

As my lips part to answer,
you use an index finger to stop my voice,
laying it across my mouth.

"Do not respond.
We will explore that next session."

Feeling a deep sense of relief
I slouch on the floor.

"Yes, Mistress."

XLVII.   *With No Words*

With no words,
I hold you tightly,
bringing your body close to mine
and sharing my energy with you.

Through the strength of my arms,
I remind you of your beauty;
of your resilience;
of your grace.

I hold you because I need you;
Because my world is better with you in it;
Because you make everything worthwhile.
I hold you because I love you.

XLVIII.   *Worship*

Wait...
Wait there.
Don't shower yet.

I know you just got back from the gym.

I just...
I just want to look at you.
Just for a second.
Let me absorb your beauty.

Look at your sloppy, carefree pony tail.
Do you know how sexy that is?

Hold on.
You have a stray strand,
It escaped your hair tie.

Here.
I'll push it back into place.

I love the definition of your arms
and the curves of your body.
Would it be ok to hold you?

I don't care if you are sweaty.
You smell amazing.

I love sweat's salty residue.
May I taste it on your neck?
Yes?

Let me undress you:
Lift your arms,
take off that t-shirt.
Help me with your sports bra.

Look at your perky breasts.
I love how the firm teardrop shape
highlights the pinkness of your nipples.

Do you prefer the left one?
Me too.

Look how hard it stands.
May I swirl my tongue around its base?

Lean against the wall.

No.
Not yet.
Leave your yoga pants on...
...for now.

Let me genuflect before you.

See how the fabric embraces you;
It loves your shape too!

Open your legs for me:
Not too wide.
Just slightly.

May I kiss your lips through the fabric?
Let my tongue trace your covered chalice?

I feel your pulse flutter
and taste your scent:
It's wild, exhilarating, and intoxicating!

Turn around.

I love the shape of your ass.
It's an inverted heart...
Perfect!

Push it out a bit.

Pull down your yoga pants.

Slowly.
Not too fast.

I want to eat you.
May I?

I feel your heat radiate on my face.

Your lips part open.
Their creaminess beckons me.

I'm going to tongue-fuck you.

Your primal essence coats my mouth.
I want you to taste yourself.
Will you kiss me?

Eat my lips like I ate you.
Take every drop.

May I give you a bath?

Take my hand,
and I will guide you.

I'm here to take care of you.

XLIX. *Your Beauty Imprints*

Your beauty imprints my psyche.
Your heart burns my soul.

Your love washes over me,
freeing me from life's enmity.

Our spirits are tethered.
I feel your mind's embrace.

You fill life with meaning,
giving me a purpose.

I want to give you the world,
but can only offer myself.

I give you my intellect and my being;
I give you my love.

I feel the universe leading me home.
Home to your arms.

L. *Kissing You Is Perfect*

Kissing you is perfect.

I love the shape of your mouth
and the intimacy of your lips.

I love sucking your tongue
and its firmness in my mouth.

I love breathing your breath
and tasting your essence.

I love the feel of your body
and the reaction of mine.

Your lips deserve worship,
and I want to conduct the service.

I want to kiss you every day.

LI.   *Want to Play a Game?*

I

We arrive at a quarter to eight.
Running a little late, but, it's okay,
they always hold our reservations.

Turning the key to off,
I listen to the engine tick as it cools
and lean over to kiss you.

As my lips caress yours,
I absorb your exotic scent:
a woody lilac swirling with notes of spring.

Exiting the car,
I walk around to the passenger side
and open your door.

You grasp my extended hand,
exert slight pressure,
and pull yourself out of the low seat.

As your legs part,
a coy smile graces your lips
and I catch a glimpse of heaven.

Standing with a twirl and a spin,
your black strappy dress
floats like a gossamer cloud.

Making sure everything is in place
and straightening your attire,
you give me a teasing look.

Hand in hand we stroll into the entrance.
I feel the passion of your body
through your clutching fingers.

We are led to our waiting table:
Close to the wall, slightly secluded,
lit by a flickering flame.

A chilled bottle of Rosé Imperial
stands in an ornate ice bucket
with a pair of crystal flutes.

Popping the cork with a twist of my wrist,
I pour the sparkling nectar in a flowing arc
and watch the bubbles rise to the surface.

To celebrate the moment,
we drink a toast to one another,
and clink our glasses together.

Drowning in your honeyed gaze,
I smile, lean forward, and ask,
"Do you want to play a game?"

As a blush blossoms on your cheeks,
you moisten your lips with your tongue,
and whisper, "Yes."

II

Don't be nervous.

I know the restaurant is busy,
but no one is watching us.
We are hidden back here.

Reach down to the hem of your dress,
pull it over your thighs—
all the way to your waist.

Slowly open your legs...
just a little wider.

I love it when you tease!

Look me in the eyes.
I want to connect with you
and swim deep in your soul.

Start with your palms on your knees,
run them up your legs,
and let your fingers linger at your crotch.
Do you feel your pulsating heat?

Wait.

The waitress just gave us a look.
I think she knows what we're doing.

Does that turn you on?

Would you like her to crawl under the table,
slide her tongue up your inner thigh,
and eat you?

No?

Good.
I am greedy and do not want to share.

Make a fist with your right hand
and extend your first two fingers.

Place them over your mons,
follow the pubic pathway to your lips,
and, through your black silk panties,
stroke your crevasse.

Move in a rhythmic pattern,
up and down with slight pressure,
tease your clit 'til it swells.

Breathe...
Breathe deep.
Let your energy flow,
and feel your chakras open.

Your nipples create fabric mountains
over your swollen breasts,
and your cheeks become flush.

Move your fingers beneath your panties
and slide them inside,
like a smooth piston in a lubed shaft.

Do not fight your feelings.
Let the moans escape your body
in time with your internal rhythm.

Using your left hand,
pull your underwear aside.
I want to watch as your fingers fuck you.

Your body shudders as you come.
An exploding orgasm ends your journey,
gushing over your digits.

I extract your hand from your panties,
bring it to my mouth,
and suck each finger clean,
swallowing your essence.

Such sweetness!

III

Recovering from our game,
your natural perfume permeates the air
as you shuffle your dress back in place.

You try to grasp the refilled flute,
but your hand trembles
with aftershocks of pleasure.

Drinking a new toast,
we celebrate your beauty
and the culmination of your delight.
Our glasses sound like crystal bells.

With a sidelong glance from the waitress,
our streaks arrive sizzling in butter:
Ravenous, we devour our meals with reckless abandon.

LII. *Animal Lust*

As a thin sheet molds to your body,
I trace your contours with my eyes:

Traveling from your gorgeous face,
I light on tented nipples
over a muscular stomach
and around curvy hips.
I flow across your mons pubis
and down shapely legs.

I love you, your mind and beauty,
but, at this moment,
I need your physicality.

As I reach with both hands,
all my weariness flees,
burned away by my boiling passion.

With a fervid pull,
I rip the sheet to the floor.

Your eyes open in wide surprise,
watching me in anticipation.

Shackling each ankle with my hands,
I spread your legs and dive face first.

My tongue pierces your veil,
and I find life's meaning.
You taste of morning dew.

As pleasure builds,
you squirm and tremble
as waves of intensity radiate to your core.

Dislodging my face,
I wipe my chin
and turn you over.

Grabbing your hips in a double grip,
I pull you to your knees.
You perch on all fours,
looking at me over your shoulder.

I smack your ass with an open palm,
and you moan as each sharp spank
paints a red glow on your porcelain skin.

Freeing myself from a fabric prison,
I tease your lips with my throbbing tool.

Heat radiates as I find your opening.
Slowly traversing your silky pathway,
I feel your heartbeat around my cock.

Holding your hips as handles,
I pull you towards me.

Steadily increasing my rhythm
and moving at a faster clip,
our slapping flesh creates sonic ripples.

With my mind in an ecstatic state,
I almost cum inside you,
but at the last moment, I pullout,
and let go over your bottom.

Breathless and dripping sweat,
I bend down and kiss your back,
tasting your salty skin.

Tracing your spine with my tongue,
I come upon your coccyx
and lick up my liquid pearls,
eating each and every drop.

I replenish my breath
and our fragrance fills my olfactory:
a sweet perfume.

You lie on your side,
bringing your knees to your chest,
and I mold my body around you,
fusing with your shape.

My animal lust sated,
I enjoy the warmth of your body
as we drift into Morpheus' arms.

LIII. *I Feel Your Spirit Flow*

I feel your spirit flow through me,
filling my cracks
and making me whole.

You heal my soul
and feed my creativity.

You are my desire
and my life goal.
I love you.

LIV. *Supplication*

You are Athena
and Aphrodite incarnate,
deserving worship.

I kneel before you
and bow my head,
awaiting your pleasure.

You gaze down at me,
golden orbs glinting,
and I feel your power.

Reaching into my chest,
I rip out my heart,
giving you everything I own.

I hope to be worthy of you.

LV. *Hope*

As I head towards oblivion,
leading an empty life,
you act as a beacon,
filling me with hope.

I see your light pulsating
over the horizon—
just out of reach.

I trudge towards you,
always moving forward
and keeping my focus.

You are an angel
sent to inspire
and to help me create.

Your touch is manna,
Life-sustaining.
Your kiss,
it's pinnacle.

You are my grail,
the quest of my life,
giving meaning to my existence.

LVI. *Dreaming*

I feel the curves of your body.
My hands trace your hips.

I love the touch of your skin,
warm and inviting,
and the press of your lips.

I travel my memory
searching for you
and exploring every facet.

I miss you in the present
and the future is uncertain,
but I know how I feel.

I dream of making you my forever girl.
Kneeling before you in worship,
I slide a ring on your finger.

A ring to praise your beauty,
A ring of my devotion,
A ring surrounding our rite.

LVII. *Transcendence*

After a long day,
I insert my key into the lock
and open the door.

With a twist of the switch,
the lamp clicks,
but nothing happens;
The electric is off.

I see a faint flicker float
as a flame moves down the hallway,
coming towards me in a steady gait.

You carry a candle,
its taper illuminating around you,
causing your skin to glow otherworldly.

Your golden eyes aflame
mirror the candle's light.

Reddish brown hair frames your face,
highlighting your ruby lips;
cascading to your shoulders.

As I watch the supple movement
of your flowing body,
I lose my breath.

You motion for me to bend down.
Your mouth tickles my ear
as a whisper plays on my drum.

"Do you love me?"

"Yes."

"Then come whip me.
I want to be punished."

As we enter the dungeon room,
it is alight with wall sconces,
melting wax pools on the slate floor.

Leaning against the wall,
a wooden x-shaped rack
with iron rings awaits us.

Placing the candle on a side table,
you turn towards me.
Your words ooze with a sensual sizzle
as they pour from your mouth.
"Strip me."

I pull your black strappy dress
up over your head
and toss it in pile to the sofa.

Your hand sized globes swell
and your pink medallions harden
as they come in contact with the raw air.

Unable to help myself,
I place my mouth on your nipple and suck,
my tongue flicking your perky tower.

With a moan building in your throat,
I disengage from my repast.

Following your curves with my hands,
I move down your hips,
over your stomach,
and slide my fingers
into the elastic band of your panties,
pulling them down to your ankles.

Your freshly shaven mons beckons me,
but I resist my urge to feast,
and help you step out of your underwear.

Your body is a muscular temple—
My favorite place to worship:
Arms and shoulders coil with tension.
Your legs, thighs, and calves, statuesque.

"Tie the ropes tightly.
I want to feel them burn."

Threading the hemp
into intricate knots,
I tie a cuff on each wrist
with rope streamers
hanging to the floor.

You release a small grunt
with each little pull.

I place you on the rack
facing the wall,
your arms extending upward.

Inserting the streamers into the rings,
I pull them tight,
making you immobile.

Stepping back, I admire your physique:
Your bare flesh contrasts
with the dark wood.
Your legs, an inverted V,
lead to your beautifully rounded bottom.

Opening my hand to a flat surface,
I rush forward
and slap your left buttock.

As your firm flesh is imprinted,
the sting vibrates on my palm
and shutters through your body.

Standing by your side,
I cup your left breast
and squeeze your nipple
while spanking alternating cheeks;
Your body trembles,
radiating pleasure and pain.

To soothe the redness,
I liberally apply aloe,
kneading it into your flesh.
You shiver from the coolness.

Gathering your hair to drape over your back,
I stroke it with a boar bristle brush,
counting to one hundred.
The steady rhythm calms us.

I leave your muscled back bare,
and kiss your neck.
In a soft whisper, I say,
"Are you ready?"

You nod yes.

I remove the flog from the wall
and feel its heft in my hand.
A spray of black leather sprouts
into forty strands from a wrapped handle.

Tracing your spine
with my left thumb,
I caress your back
while softly bouncing the leather
over your arms and legs.
Goosebumps spring over your body.

With a sharp flick of my wrist...
KA-rak!
I strike your shoulder
and rub the sting away.

"Again!"

KA-Rak!
into your thigh.

"Harder!"

KA-RAK!
The center of your back.

"Hit me again!"

KA-Rak!
Across your butt.

"Damn it!
Hit me harder!"

I swirl the flog twice
around my head,
KA-Rak!
KA-RAK!!
KA-RAKK!!!

As you cry out
gripping the rack,
red welts swell,
rising on your porcelain skin.

I drop the flog to the floor
and rub a salve over your body,
massaging away the hurt
and the tension.

With a pull of the slip knot,
I untie you from the rack
and you flow into my arms.

Carrying you to the sofa,
I wrap you in swaddling.

Through your pain,
we bring our awareness
to a higher level.

Going to my knees,
I bend over you,
and kiss your cheeks, nose, and lips,
tasting the saltiness of your tears.

LVIII. *You Are my Queen*

You are my Queen.

As royalty,
you hold important treasures:
My heart,
my soul,
my inspiration.

I hope to do you justice
as I continue questing.

LIX. *Fucking*

I love finger fucking you.
My fingers pump inside you
as my thumb rubs your clit.

I travel your smooth velvet corridor,
each thrust pushing you towards ecstasy.

Your body writhes,
your breath sighs,
and your eyes rotate white.

As I kneel between your spread legs,
a hand in you
and the other stroking my shaft.
I move forward
and trace your lips with my head.

Blood gorges and throbs in both of us.
Our heat intermingles.

I find your opening and push.
I feel the comforting tightness
as your cunt grips my veiny tower.

Your eyes open wide,
and you mouth lets out an "Oh God."

Using your hips as handles, I hold tight,
and gyrate in a pumping rhythm.

I gain speed as lubrication flows.
My cock becomes coated creamy white,
and our sex fills my nostrils.

My movement increases
as your moans punctuate
the slapping of our flesh.

All thought leaves my brain
and a primal urge takes over.
I feel my balls tightening
and pressure building.

Your pussy is amazing!
I want to drench it in cum—
inside and out.

When everything begins to let go,
I am balls deep.
Pleasure drains through my body
and explodes towards my cock.

I realize where I am
and make a quick exit,
pulling out with a liquid pop.

I cum on your lips, mons, and stomach:
You are glazed with my fluid.

LX. *Specter of Your Beauty*

The specter of your beauty haunts,
drifting through my memories
and bringing visions of happiness.

I reach out to grasp at its wispy tentacles,
trying to recapture my past rapture.

But the once vivid visions
drift by in monochrome,
their grandeur fading.

The dreariness of life's pall
infects my waking hours
and erases past glories.

Kneeling in the twilight,
I watch as the moon rises
and brightens the celestial ceiling.

I feel your presence,
the grace of your dance,
and the radiance of your eyes.
My soul renews.

LXI. *As Midnight Darkens*

As midnight darkens,
I stand in the yard,
and gaze into the sky.

The brightness of the sun
bounces off the moon
as it reaches full flower.

Through a glorious glow,
the sphere of radiance calls to me.
It's your voice I hear.

In a familiar timbre,
I hear tones of reassurance,
and my doubts wash away.

I feel the magic of your spirit,
and see the light of your soul.
I realize the Goddess lives,
and she lives as you.

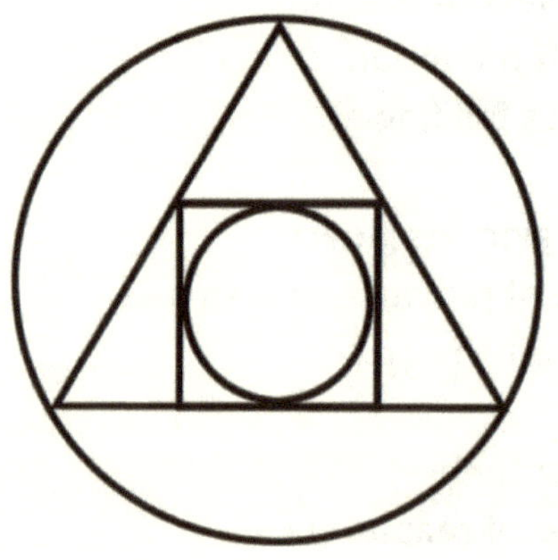

Title and Page 272
Philosopher's Stone -
Symbol of enlightenment, heavenly bliss, and perfection.

Page 6
Triple moon -
Goddess symbol for the Maiden, Mother, and Crone.

Page 24
Antimony -
Symbol for the wild and free parts of human nature.

Page 54
Phosphorus -
Symbol for illumination.

Page 138
Magnesium -
Symbol of eternity.

Sources:

http://www.crystalinks.com/triplegoddess.html

http://mythologian.net/alchemy-symbols-meanings-
extended-list-alchemical-symbols/

Acknowledgments

There are a number of people I wish to thank:

Manuela Serra for her beautiful cover.
It captures the essence of my book.

Eva Zen's precise editing and comments helped me to
make the manuscript shine.

Georgia and Rayna for reading my manuscript and their
kind words.

My longtime friend, Olivia, for her invaluable support
and encouragement.

And I wish to thank my muse, Anna.
Without her inspiration this collection would not exist.

Andrew Chiniche has lived in Hawaii, the Virgin Islands, and Florida, but his favorite place is in the worlds of books and movies. He believes every work of fiction contains truth hidden in the wonderful and fantastic.

Andrew received a degree in English Literature from Mississippi State University, and currently lives in Alabama.